"Jayne, _with me tonight?_"

She headed for her desk. "I'm free, but let me check with Mr. Waterman. I know he'd like to be there...."

Garrett stepped forward and covered her hand with his. "I don't want to have dinner with Jayne, the accountant," he said near her ear. "I want to have dinner with Jayne, the woman."

Jayne, the woman, was flabbergasted. "You do?"

Garrett laughed softly. "Is that so hard to believe?"

"Well...yes."

"Why? We've spent days working long hours together and I'd like to get to know you better."

He made having dinner with her sound so logical. Jayne excelled at logic. "I'd love to."

Texan **Heather MacAllister** lives with her electrical-engineer husband and two live-wire sons whose antics inspire her humorous take on love and life. She writes for both Harlequin Romance® and Harlequin® Temptation®, finding that the main difference between her stories for each is that the Romance heroines find love, but love finds the Temptation heroines. And of course, they all live happily ever after.

Books by Heather MacAllister

HARLEQUIN ROMANCE

*written as Heather Allison

The Boss and the
Plain Jayne Bride
Heather MacAllister

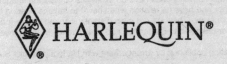

HARLEQUIN®

TORONTO • NEW YORK • LONDON
AMSTERDAM • PARIS • SYDNEY • HAMBURG
STOCKHOLM • ATHENS • TOKYO • MILAN • MADRID
PRAGUE • WARSAW • BUDAPEST • AUCKLAND

ISBN 0-373-03555-1

THE BOSS AND THE PLAIN JAYNE BRIDE

First North American Publication 1999.

Copyright © 1999 by Heather W. MacAllister.

CHAPTER ONE

"ONE hundred twenty-three thousand dollars sitting in a dormant account?" Tilting back in the executive chair, Mr. Waterman raised a silver eyebrow. "I see you've been your usual diligent self, Jayne."

"Just doing my job." Until recently—until last night, in fact—the dry acknowledgment from Jayne Nelson's boss would have made all the sacrificed evenings of the past week worth it. But yesterday had been her twenty-eighth birthday, and she'd spent it working overtime instead of celebrating with her friend Sylvia.

The thrill of getting faint praise from the senior partner at Pace Waterman Accountants was gone, vanishing about the same time she bit into her fourth chocolate-frosted cupcake, left over from the ones Sylvia had brought to the coffee room to mark her birthday. They'd gone stale, rather like her life.

"Nevertheless, Brock Neilson's widow has every reason to be grateful I designated you as her accountant." Mr. Waterman casually tossed the file he'd been examining onto the desk.

Jayne tried to remain detached, difficult since the file represented hours of tedious work.

"How did you know to look for those CDs when no one else did?" he asked.

No one else had wanted to put in the effort of auditing the past tax returns. It was a waste of time, the other accountants had told her. But Jayne had suspected something was wrong and decided to pursue her hunch on her own. It wasn't the first time she'd done so, and it wouldn't be the last, which was why, at the relatively tender age of twenty-seven—make that twenty-eight—Jayne found herself poised on the threshold of a vice presidency. Unfortunately Mr. Waterman didn't want to open the door.

The unsettling thing was that she didn't care as much as she had yesterday. Maybe it was the cupcakes she'd eaten for dinner.

Jayne picked up the file she'd brought to his attention. "In 1992, there was a steep drop-off in Mr. Neilson's reported interest income, which his former accountants explained by maturing certificates of deposit. I checked and there was never any record of the CDs in his subsequent financial statements, nor was there an investment made using those funds."

Mr. Waterman shook his head. "He had two in college and one in medical school about that time. My guess is he planned to use the cash for the kids."

Jayne withheld her comment on the financially questionable decision to leave a chunk of cash sitting without drawing interest. "Anyway, there wasn't a record of this money in his financial assets when he hired Pace Waterman," she assured him.

Again Mr. Waterman shook his head. "Remarkable piece of detective work. My congratulations." He stood and offered Jayne his hand.

Just remember this at my annual review, she thought as she shook it and returned to her office.

"Amazing Jayne strikes again," said a familiar voice behind her.

Jayne grinned. "Listening at the door, Sylvia?"

"Naturally. It was open." Sylvia Dennison, a secretary with the insurance company three floors above Pace Waterman, and Jayne's best friend, fell into step beside her. She hooked a thumb over her shoulder. "Hey, that sounded pretty good back there. What did you do this time?"

Jayne tapped the file folder. "Found money for a widow."

"That was noble of you."

"And not just any widow—the widow of one of Mr. Waterman's oldest and dearest friends."

"Way to go, Jayne! Noble and self-serving at the same time." Sylvia gave her a look of approval.

Jayne pushed open the door to her office. "Must you make everything sound sordid?"

"Oh, please. Don't tell me you didn't think of it." Sylvia followed her into the office, flopped over the arm of Jayne's leather couch and swung her leg back and forth. "Anyway, I suppose it was worth spending the whole week *and* your birthday with a calculator instead of with me."

Jayne was busy clearing off her desk, but didn't miss the petulance in Sylvia's voice. "You wouldn't have noticed, except that you're between boyfriends."

"I noticed because *days* ago you promised to help me put that aubergine rinse in my hair." Sylvia patted her raven tresses.

Jayne had doubts about the aubergine, especially after the home perm Sylvia had insisted on giving her. Instead of full, shiny bouncy hair, she had brown dandelion fluff. Women accountants didn't look particularly professional with dandelion fluff for hair.

"Well, anyway, we should celebrate tonight." Sylvia bounced to her feet. "Shall we go to that new club on Richmond where the brokers hang out? Or how about the sports bar with the lawyers?"

"I can't tonight." And Jayne was glad because she hated trailing after Sylvia on her manhunting excursions into Houston's stylish restaurants. "I'm teaching the June accounting seminars."

"Jayne!" Sylvia crossed her arms and stuck out her lower lip. "Can't they give you a break? There are a ton of accountants working here. Why do you always get stuck teaching the seminars?"

"I like teaching the seminars." Jayne emptied her electric pencil sharpener into the wastebasket at the side of her desk.

"Try this equation—Jayne works nights equals Jayne never meets anyone."

"Sylvia." Jayne swept pencil shavings off her desk. "You're sounding like my mother's Sunday afternoon phone calls." And they were probably both right.

A crafty smile lit Sylvia's face. "Speaking of relatives—"

"No more blind dates!" At least not the blind dates Sylvia arranged.

"Are you still mad about Mogo?"

"As soon as I heard his name was Mogo, I should have said 'No go.'" Most of Sylvia's male relatives played sports. Mogo, aka Mogo the Magnificent, was a professional wrestler. Jayne's question about whether the matches were real or fixed proved to be the evening's conversational highlight, especially since Mogo had chosen to take her to one of his. He'd abandoned her outside the entrance to the dressing area, apparently forgetting he'd brought a date, which was fine with Jayne.

Sylvia opened her mouth, but Jayne broke in. "Want to join me for a sandwich downstairs?" Food and men were Sylvia's two favorite topics.

She groaned. "Not the company snack bar!"

"I've only got an hour before class starts."

"Jayne, let's at least go to the Greek place across the street."

Jayne laughed as she retrieved her purse from the bottom file cabinet drawer. "I thought there weren't any men who ate there."

"No eligible ones." Sylvia trudged beside her. "They work around here and I've already eliminated them as possibilities."

Ten minutes later, Jayne and Sylvia, seated in a vinyl booth next to the window, were trying to resist a bowl of salty, oily olives—Sylvia more successfully than Jayne.

"Jayne, fat and salt equal secretary's butt."

Jayne dropped the black olive. "You don't have to keep talking to me in equations."

"You're an accountant. You understand equations." Sylvia snatched the bread basket away from Jayne's creeping hand. "No bread, either!"

"I like olives! I like bread!" Jayne wailed. She inhaled, her eyes closed. "Warm, yeasty, crusty...I can smell it from here!"

The basket thudded to the table. "Heads up. New waiter."

"I suppose you're not going to let me order moussaka, either," Jayne grumbled as an attractive dark-eyed man approached.

"Perish the thought."

While Sylvia simpered at the waiter, Jayne defiantly snuck in her order for moussaka and ate an olive for good measure. Then another. She was reaching for the bread basket when she saw him.

The most gorgeous man in the universe, or at the very least in Texas, stepped from the evening sunshine into Garcia's Greek Eats. Impossibly, stunningly handsome, he paused and blinked as his eyes adjusted to the interior.

Jayne's heart hammered with such force she felt the tremor in her hands. The man was out of Sylvia's sight, or Jayne knew the waiter who had captured her friend's interest would be forgotten. In fact, when Sylvia did spot this man, she'd probably kill Jayne for not pointing him out to her earlier.

But Jayne couldn't move, couldn't breathe and didn't want to share the beautiful man, though he was so far above her orbit, he was more dream than reality.

The restaurant owner approached the sable-haired god and led him to a table on the opposite side of the room where he sat in profile to her and still behind Sylvia.

Jayne swallowed, her mouth dry and brackish from the olives.

"Jayne?" Sylvia gave her a strange look.

"What?" With difficulty, Jayne dragged her gaze away from the Gorgeous One.

"I'll bring more bread," the waiter said smoothly.

Sylvia glanced to Jayne's bread plate where three rolls and five olive pits sat.

"Oh." Jayne stared at rolls she didn't remember taking and the pits of the olives she didn't remember eating. "I'm hungry?"

With Sylvia still looking at her skeptically, Jayne bit into a roll and chewed as though she were enjoying it.

"At least you aren't slathering them with butter." As she spoke, Sylvia looked over Jayne's shoulder out the window, allowing Jayne the opportunity to stare at the man undetected.

From this distance, she couldn't make out the minute details of his appearance, but what she saw was more than enough to steal her breath. Though dressed in a casual shirt and pants, he had a sleek, well-put-together look about him.

Toying with her roll, Jayne only half listened as Sylvia extolled the virtues of exercise and fat-free dining and warned Jayne about the dangers of cellulite in women of their age. Sylvia was nearing thirty—nearer than Jayne, but Jayne knew better than to point that out.

She sighed and ate a particularly large olive. No one was likely to see her cellulite anyway.

"Don't think I didn't see you eat that olive." Sylvia interrupted her monologue. "I've a highly developed peripheral vision. Nothing much gets by me."

Except the man behind her and Jayne decided not to mention him. Once or twice, he checked his watch, but he never looked their way, of course. When the waiter approached, he ordered and appeared to be dining alone. Incredible. The woman in his life—Jayne didn't doubt there was one—shouldn't let him go out alone. If he were in Jayne's life, *she* wouldn't let him out of her sight for a minute.

Letting Sylvia's words waft around her, Jayne transported herself into the empty chair across from the man.

He'd raise his eyes to hers, greet her warmly and smile a smile just for her.

And she'd...

Jayne tried again. And she'd...she'd...

Nothing. She wouldn't do anything because she'd never have the courage to be with or even speak to a man like that.

Such a man was not for her. She acknowledged this fact without self-pity. Beautiful people were attracted to other beautiful people. That was simply a law of nature intended to protect their gene pool. Others might go swimming in that pool, but would soon find they were in over their heads. Survival of the fittest, or in this case, beautifulest.

"Jayne? Are you listening to me?"

"Nope."

"Figures." Sylvia pointed to Jayne's bread plate. "What is with you?"

Jayne stared at her fingers, which were buried in a mound of bread crumbs. "The bread was dry," she declared and withdrew her hand, scattering bread crumbs and bits of crust across the table. "Really, really dry."

"And you're really, really distracted. Are you going to tell me about it?''

"No," Jayne said as their dinner arrived, "I'm not."

How could she have eaten so much? Jayne stood in the Pace Waterman conference room and regretted each and every bite of the moussaka. Well, maybe not the first half-dozen bites, but after that she should've quit eating and would have if Sylvia hadn't been scolding her for ordering the heavy dish in the first place.

She was really cross with Sylvia because her scolding kept Jayne from daydreaming about the dreamboat. And then she had to leave the restaurant because of this seminar and didn't get a chance to see the man's full face instead of his admittedly perfect profile.

Thus, when the most gorgeous man in the universe strolled into her accounting seminar, Jayne didn't recognize him until he turned his head to speak to the dazed woman already seated in the row. Then he sat at a student desk, looking for all the world as though he thought he belonged there.

He didn't, of course. Spectacularly gorgeous men did not study accounting at seminars, at least not at the seminars sponsored by the Pace Waterman accounting firm. In general, gorgeous people did not study accounting at all. Jayne knew this, being an accountant herself.

In two minutes, she would have to start class. This meant that in two minutes, after she welcomed those present to Accounting for Small Businesses, the breathtaking man sitting three seats from the front would recognize his mistake, furrow his brow in attractive confusion, laugh an attractively self-deprecating laugh and excuse himself, attractively, from her life forever.

Jayne had two minutes to imprint every detail of his perfect features on her psyche. Two minutes to fuel future fantasies. It wasn't much, but she could work with it.

Taking a step closer, she inhaled, as if to absorb his essence into her being, and let her breath out on a sigh as her eyes traced the contours of his face.

From the cleft in his chin, her gaze climbed the steep slope of his cheekbones, waded through the blue pools of his eyes, tangled in his black brows, slid down an impossibly straight nose and landed in the valley between his lips.

His lips. Jayne shivered and clutched the class roster to the bodice of her navy-blue suit. Not skinny lips and not full, blatantly sensual lips; these lips were kissing lips. Athletic lips.

Jayne had never been privileged to kiss or be kissed by such a pair of lips. And even if a man of her acquaintance possessed such lips, he wouldn't know what to do with them. Jayne doubted she would know what to do with them, either, but she was willing to learn.

Her watch beeped the hour. Lost in the valley of the shadow of his lips, Jayne tried to ignore the beep but a restless shifting and a few stray whispers among the two dozen people seated before her told her she'd better start class.

Drawing a breath, she spoke the words which would send the stunning god back to Mount Olympus. "Welcome to Small Business Accounting sponsored by the accounting firm of Pace Waterman. I'm Jayne Nelson, your instructor.'' She paused, waiting for him to leave.

He regarded her with an impassive blue gaze.

''We'll be meeting twice a week for six weeks,'' she continued, and looked at him expectantly.

He smiled a politely devastating smile. He had dimples. Jayne smothered her small whimper before it could escape.

''I'll call roll, so I can get to know you.'' *Please be on the list. Please be on the list.*

Suppressing the impulse to skip all the female names, Jayne began at the top of the alphabet and was rewarded when a deep male voice answered, ''Here'' to the name Garrett Charles.

Garrett Charles. Jayne Nelson Charles. Jayne Charles. Jaynie Charles. Mrs. Garrett Charles. She sighed and raced through the rest of the roster.

He was on the list. He had actually paid money to take the class. He *belonged* here. The accounting gods were smiling on her.

Pace Waterman offered a variety of courses and seminars such as this one geared toward people who were thinking of starting their own businesses. Naturally Pace Waterman hoped that the business would grow and eventually require the services of one of their accountants, especially during income tax season.

The account executives took turns teaching the seminars and this was Jayne's rotation.

Lucky Jayne.

She set the roster on the table, remembering to suck in her moussaka-laden stomach.

"Ninety percent of all start-up businesses fail within one year due to lack of sufficient operating capital," she began, wondering what kind of business Garrett Charles was in. He looked like the restaurant type.

Why don't you ask him? "I'm going to go around the room and have each of you tell a little about the business you have or plan to start. Then I can tailor the class more to your needs." *I'm good. I'm really, really good.*

Boutiques, bookstores, craft stores, a couple of fast-food franchises, restaurants and...

"I'm taking over the family modeling agency," he said.

Of course. She should have known that Garrett Charles was either a model or an actor.

A feminine purr greeted his announcement as the women unconsciously straightened spines and hair. The men wore varying looks of disdain and threatened manhood.

Jayne's stomach muscles hurt. "I don't know anything about the modeling business," she blurted out. *He knows that. All he has to do is look at you. You're five-three and...curvy. And why did you let Sylvia give you a home perm?*

"And I don't know anything about the accounting business." Garrett stretched those gorgeous kissable lips of his into a smile that revealed teeth so straight and white they wouldn't need retouching in a photograph. His dimples deepened and Jayne's knees quivered. "I suppose that makes us even."

Even. She was even with a man who could look good in fluorescent lighting.

"And I don't know anything about this accounting stuff, either, but I sure would like to," prompted one of Jayne's male students. "So let's get on with it, already."

She couldn't remember the man's name because she hadn't been paying attention when she called roll.

Turning to the man, Garrett presented his perfect profile to Jayne. "And what business are you in, Mr....?"

"Name's Monty. My mother-in-law is coming from Italy to live with the wife and me. She likes to cook." He shrugged. "Friend of mine, he's got a restaurant down in Montrose and he's ready to retire. I got a mother-in-law who needs something to do. I figured, let her cook." Monty spread his hands. "So I bought the place."

"And then you found out about the paperwork, right?" Garrett's eyebrows arched.

Monty made a disgusted sound. "You ain't kiddin'."

Garrett had deflected Monty's heckling and Jayne fell a little bit in love with him for it. However, this was her class and she could handle herself.

"Most of you are probably feeling overwhelmed by the financial records you must keep for the government." There was murmured agreement. "That's exactly why Pace Waterman recommends that you take this overview. Then afterward, when you meet with one of our account executives, you'll be able to make an informed decision about whether or not you need further assistance." And naturally, Pace Waterman was standing by to offer that assistance, which an average of thirty-seven percent of the people finishing the seminar accepted—and paid for. The rest either dropped out, decided that owning their own business wasn't such a good idea after all or actually did their own bookkeeping. Rarely did they contact another accounting firm, a fact Pace Waterman used to justify subsidizing the courses.

Jayne removed a stack of papers from the table and passed them out. "This is a schedule of the subjects we'll discuss. If you miss a topic, you may come to that session during another seminar."

While the class rustled the papers, Jayne distributed the course notebooks, vinyl binders with the Pace Waterman logo prominently featured. Jayne's distaste for the relentless self-promotion was offset by the valuable information contained in the binders. Informed clients were satisfied clients was the Pace Waterman philosophy, to which Jayne heartily subscribed.

The binders were on a small cart that Jayne wheeled around the room.

She was going to see Garrett Charles up close. Would he be just as devastatingly attractive? Would there be some minute flaw in his appearance? Jayne refused to look his way until she was actually handing him his notebook.

He glanced up to smile his thanks and Jayne's gaze collided with his. Her breath caught. She couldn't move. She barely felt him slide the binder out of her nerveless fingers. The Pace Waterman mint-green and burgundy conference room ceased to exist as Jayne lost herself in the marvel that was Garrett Charles.

He had beautiful skin the color of buttery leather with the slightest darkening above his upper lip. She inhaled and was pleased to discover that he wore no scent.

"Thank you." His deep voice broke the spell that paralyzed her.

Flushing, Jayne lurched toward the next student.

And bashed the cart into Garrett's knee.

She knew it the instant she felt the bump. "I'm so sorry!" she gasped as he grimaced.

But it was an elegant, manly grimace, quickly smoothed.

"No." He waved away her apology and briefly massaged his leg. "I should have moved my foot out of the aisle."

"But it must hurt!" Jayne knelt to inspect the damage, brushing at the place on his khaki-clad thigh where the cart had left a dark smudge.

"It's fine now. Really." He placed his hand directly over hers.

Jayne stared at the well-shaped hand with its ringless fingers covering hers. She felt the muscles of his leg tense under her fingers and in that instant, became fully aware of her position. His waist and points south were directly in her line of sight and her hand was on the hard muscles of his thigh.

Meeting his faintly amused blue eyes, Jayne gasped a horrified, "Ohmigosh!", shot to her feet and blindly pushed the cart.

There was a shuffling sound as the rest of the students drew in their legs. Behind her, Jayne knew at least three feet separated the cart from the next row of desks. Plenty of room, unless one were trying to get as close as possible to Garrett Charles, which she had been.

Parking the cart in the front, Jayne gathered her tattered composure and faced the class. "If any of you had concerns about your personal safety during the class, I believe I've sufficiently demonstrated my proficiency with the rolling cart—" she gave it a pat "—a vastly underrated weapon."

Soft laughter broke the tension, but Jayne didn't know how she got through the next two hours, or even what she said. Every time she looked at Garrett, she was in danger of losing her place in the lesson, so she had to concentrate more than usual. By the time she dismissed class, she had a headache.

Resting her forehead against the dry erase board prior to cleaning it, Jayne didn't realize at first that she had company.

"Are you all right?" asked a deep male voice behind her.

She whirled around, then jammed the heel of her hand against her head as the pain speared through it. "Uh, I've got a headache," she managed to say even though voices in her poor abused head were shouting at her to say something witty.

His brow furrowed in attractive wrinkles. *Attractive wrinkles* for Pete's sake. "I'm sorry." He sounded as though he meant it. Good trick. "I noticed that you seemed distracted this evening," he began diplomatically, "and I hope it wasn't because you felt awkward about bumping me with the cart."

Bumping. How kind he was. "I am *so* sorry about that. How's your leg? It's bruised, isn't it?" she asked, when he hesitated.

"Don't worry about it." A corner of his mouth

tilted upward, deepening a dimple. "Accidents happen."

"That's very generous of you."

"Why? You're telling me it wasn't an accident?"

Jayne's eyes widened. "Of course it was!" she spluttered, horrified.

Garrett laughed lightly and touched her briefly on the shoulder. "Relax. I'm kidding. I only wanted you to know that I'm not the kind of person who'll have his lawyer camping on your doorstep within twenty-four hours, in case you were worried."

Jayne's mouth opened. She'd never even considered that he might sue. Her financial life flashed before her.

He raised an eyebrow. "Everything okay?"

Jayne shut her mouth and, having lost the power of speech, nodded.

"See you on Thursday, then." He turned and walked out of the conference room, footsteps muffled by the industrial carpeting.

Jayne stared after him. He was coming back! She was going to get a second chance!

So what was she going to do with it?

CHAPTER TWO

JAYNE might as well have stayed at home for all the work she accomplished the next day. What happened to competence? Disgusted with herself, she thumbed through the reports left over from yesterday and sighed. Garrett Charles was haunting her every waking moment and most of her sleeping ones as well.

Over and over, she relived the embarrassing moments from last night. She'd stared at him, attacked him with the book cart and then lectured on who knows what. Her only hope was that since she'd taught the class so many times, her brain could coast for a while. She hoped it was coasting in familiar waters.

Then there was the strange, unsettled feeling she'd had lately. She probably needed a vacation. That was it. Maybe she could talk Sylvia into one of those four-day cruises that left from the Port of Houston. At the prospect, Jayne immediately felt brighter.

That was it. She just needed a vacation. Her life had become drab and predictable and her reaction to Garrett was nature's way of telling her that her social life needed attention. A lot of attention. Her mother had always told her she was going to be a late bloomer. Well, twenty-eight was late and Jayne must be blooming.

On Thursday, class day, Jayne stood indecisively in front of her closet. What to wear, what to wear.

Her sartorial decisions usually consisted of which version of a navy-blue suit she would wear. Solid? Midnight-navy? Royal-blue navy? Pin-striped? Glen-plaid? White blouse or pale blue? Blue on red tie or red on blue? She'd always been pleased with her professional wardrobe. Now it all looked too...too something. Predictable? Staid? Stuffy? All of the above?

There was always her beige suit, which she wore in the heat of summer, but she felt like a lightweight in it.

Okay, she'd analyze the situation. She wanted to appear competent to reassure everyone after Tuesday, so she'd wear her most conservative, expensive, darkest suit with a blinding white shirt and a regimental striped women's ascot at the neck. She'd add height with her highest heeled pumps.

She set off for work, feeling her old competent self. It was a good feeling and one she wanted to hold on to until her vacation.

"Hey, Jayne, you look ready to take on the world," commented Bill Pellman as she passed his cubicle on the way to her office. "Big account on the line?"

"No," Jayne responded with deliberate casualness, "but I do have class to teach tonight."

Bill was young, eager and considered Jayne his mentor—a pleasant, sexless mentor who lived for work just as he did. Jayne sighed, thinking there was more truth there than she liked.

"Any hot prospects?" he asked now.

She thought of Garrett and her throat went dry. "Not really," she croaked and fled to her office.

So much for renewed competence. Just thinking of

Garrett made her heart race, so she attempted to figure out her surprising response to him.

Never in her life had she responded to a man's physical appearance with such…awareness. Parts of her body, parts that were usually hibernating, had awakened. She wasn't even sure she was experiencing desire. Desire flourished when there was a chance of being desired in return. Competent, realistic, feet-firmly-on-the-ground Jayne Nelson did not attract the Garrett Charles type of man. Her head knew that, but her body must have short-circuited. That would explain the tingling.

She was staring off into the distance, chewing on a pen, when Sylvia popped into her office.

"I've got a Schlotz's Deli two-for-one coupon. You interested?"

Jayne dropped her pen. "Is it time for lunch already?"

Sylvia held up her arm, which was decorated with three gaudy watches.

"Oh. Right." Jayne pushed back her chair and pulled her purse from the file drawer.

"Aren't you going to change your shoes?" Sylvia kicked out a sneaker-clad foot.

"Shoes?" Jayne blinked.

"The deli is at the other end of the mall by the movie theater."

"Oh. Right. I should change." Pace Waterman was in the Transco Tower, which was connected by a walkway to Houston's Galleria mall across the street. Jayne and Sylvia frequently spent their lunch hours hiking through it for exercise.

Jayne stood staring at the bank of file drawers.

Where was Garrett's business? She hadn't thought to ask. What if he opened the agency right in the mall? She might see him all the time now. She sighed.

Sylvia came into the room, gently opened the supply cabinet and removed Jayne's walking shoes. "What's up, Jayne?"

"Nothing." Jayne slipped out of her pumps and worked her feet into the sneakers. She felt her face grow warm, so she bent to tie the shoes, hoping any evidence of a blush might be hidden.

"You're acting just like you did the other night. Are you feeling okay? Have you got an audit or something this afternoon?"

"I'm fine!"

"Then...Jayne?" Sylvia nudged her arm. "Have you met somebody?" she asked in a tone that meant "Have you met a man?"

"No!" Jayne responded too quickly and too loudly. She could tell by the triumphant smirk on Sylvia's face. Drat. Now Sylvia would worm everything out of her. Sylvia could worm anything out of anybody. She was wasted in secretarial work. Her true calling was espionage.

Jayne crossed her purse over her shoulder bandolier-style and Sylvia linked their arms. "I want you to tell me *everything*," she demanded.

"There's nothing to tell," Jayne protested feebly.

Sylvia patted her arm. "Why don't you let me be the judge of that?"

Sylvia had wormed everything there was to worm by the time they reached the elevator.

"That's *it?*" She snorted in disgust as they exited

the elevator and made their way through the crowded
foyer toward the walkway.

"I told you there wasn't anything to tell," Jayne
pointed out, secretly hoping that Sylvia might put a
hopeful spin on the events of Tuesday night. But not
even Sylvia could interpret rendering succor after
bashing someone in the leg as flirting.

"But I didn't actually *believe* you." Sylvia
frowned, then shrugged. "No matter. We'll find you
a man yet. In fact..." She cocked her head to one
side.

"No," Jayne refused automatically. Sylvia was
continually trotting out male relatives for Jayne to
date.

And sure enough... "My second cousin Vincent is
going to be in his roommate's wedding in Galveston.
He'll be staying with my aunt Ida a couple of nights.
Why don't I—"

"No." Jayne closed her eyes against the thought
of dating Sylvia's second-tier relatives.

"Then ask out the man in your class."

Jayne swallowed her automatic "no" and mentally
tested the idea of asking out Garrett Charles.

Not possible. "I probably shouldn't date students."
She walked faster.

"He'll only be a student for a few weeks. You're
just too wimpy," Sylvia scolded, jogging to keep up
with her.

"I know."

"Men *like* assertive women."

Jayne shot her an exasperated look. "On what
planet?"

"Uh, Planet Eros?"

"See? Aliens."

"Speaking of, how about I set you up with Vincent?"

"Sylvia!"

She shrugged. "You gotta kiss a lot of frogs before you find a prince."

"For the last time, I do not want to go out with your alien frog second cousin!"

However... Jayne stopped abruptly and snagged Sylvia's arm. They'd reached the end of the mall walkway and were standing right by the travel agency they'd walked past on a hundred other lunch hours.

"What? What?"

Jayne pointed to a bright poster advertising fun in the Gulf of Mexico. "I think I need a vacation. Or a change in my life. A vacation *would* be a change in my life." She turned to the gaping Sylvia. "I was thinking we could book one of those four-day cruises. They're not very expen—"

"Yes!" Sylvia had recovered from her astonishment and was pushing Jayne through the double glass doors and straight over to the brochure display. "This is the *best* idea you've ever had!" She started taking two of every brochure with a ship pictured on it, handing one to Jayne as she babbled.

"When do you want to leave? Can we wait until I lose five pounds? What if we save up and go for a seven-day cruise? We'll have to watch which line we pick." She stopped gabbing long enough to flip through one of the brochures. "There are even singles cruises. We should go on one of those to increase the odds. Okay. I think we've got one of each." She smiled brightly at Jayne. "Let's go eat."

Sylvia's enthusiasm was infectious and they window-shopped through the mall all the way to the deli. Jayne followed Sylvia inside where she was nearly overwhelmed by the pastrami and pickle smell.

Sylvia inhaled rapturously, then sighed. "This will be our last pastrami on rye until after the cruise."

"It will?" Jayne asked, a little overwhelmed by how fast and hard Sylvia had latched onto the cruise idea.

"We'll have to start dieting immediately." Sylvia flashed a big smile at a group of jacketless men, who scooted down on the benches, making room for the two of them. Or more precisely, for the vibrant Sylvia, who beckoned to Jayne.

Jayne was accepted only because it was obvious Sylvia wouldn't sit without her. She sighed, but sat down on the bench just the same.

By the time the men left a couple of minutes later, Sylvia had collected three business cards.

Jayne leafed through her brochures and tried not to feel envious.

"So which ships look good?" Sylvia asked as she tossed two business cards into the ashtray and wrote a note to herself on the back of the third.

"I want to stick to the one that leaves out of Houston," Jayne said. "It's more convenient." She found the cruise line's brochure in Sylvia's stack.

They paged through it until their sandwiches arrived. Just as Sylvia closed the brochure, Jayne caught a glimpse of compelling blue eyes. Blue eyes she'd sworn she'd seen before.

This was sick. She was obsessing about Garrett, imagining she saw him everywhere. Nevertheless, her heart picked up speed as she opened her own copy. She'd either find those eyes or she'd better start looking for a therapist.

Paying no attention at all to Sylvia's chatter, Jayne searched the brochure, locating him immediately.

Garrett Charles was one of the people posing as passengers for the cruise line. Several of the group were in one of the deck lounges holding drinks with pineapple spears and tiny umbrellas. Garrett and another man stood at the railing nearby. He wore an open neck knit shirt that exposed his throat and just enough chest hair to send Jayne into a near swoon. And that was before she noticed his muscle definition. Once she saw those pecs, Jayne was a goner. Khaki shorts revealed his legs. Or his legs as they'd appeared before Jayne had bashed one with the book cart.

And then she found the picture of Garrett by the pool.

"So what do you say, Jayne?" Sylvia asked.

"Yes, sure," Jayne mumbled, intent on getting back to the office as soon as possible so she could spend the rest of the afternoon staring at a shirtless Garrett. Maybe if she stared long enough, she'd get over him. He was only a man, for heaven's sake.

But it didn't work, probably because Garrett was no ordinary man. All staring at his pictures accomplished, other than making her fall behind in her project schedule, was to make her nervous about that evening's class.

She couldn't do it. She couldn't chance another disaster. She'd find somebody else to teach the rest of Accounting for Small Businesses. Somebody who wouldn't turn into a bundle of lusting nerves at the sight of Garrett Charles. Somebody like...

"Bill, think of this as an opportunity to acquire new accounts." Jayne spoke in her most mentorlike voice. "I've been analyzing your performance during the first half of this fiscal year, and I believe you're ready to handle one of the recruitment classes."

"You think so?" The expression of doubt Bill had worn since Jayne first broached the subject of teaching her classes faded.

Jayne leaned a well-padded hip against his desk and crossed her arms over her chest. "People equate age with experience—"

"That's why you dress the way you do," Bill interrupted, nodding his understanding.

"What do you mean?" Jayne straightened and looked down at herself. "What's wrong with the way I dress?"

"Nothing. It's very effective. Isn't that what I said?"

"Effective for what?"

"Jayne." Bill grimaced with impatience. "Clients look at you and see that you're all business." He gestured with his hand. "Suit, shirt and tie equals business."

"Oh." Jayne was placated—

"Nobody would ever guess you're as young as you are."

—until that crack. She gritted her teeth.

"So you think these classes are a way I can nab some new accounts?" asked the oblivious Bill.

"Yes," Jayne assured him with less enthusiasm

than before. "Since you're young and inexperienced," she enjoyed pointing out, "this is a way to demonstrate your competence to potential clients."

"Could be cool." Bill nodded to himself then announced, "Okay, I'll do it, but I can't tonight—"

Jayne panicked. "You *have* to! I mean, I have plans."

"Oh?" He drew out the syllable and eyed her speculatively. "What sort of plans?"

"Private plans," she said with an edge of desperation.

Bill raised an eyebrow and Jayne felt herself flush. "So it wasn't strictly my stellar performance that prompted this burst of generosity?"

"I..." Jayne gave up. "Not entirely, no, but I wouldn't have asked you if I hadn't thought you were ready," she said in a version of the truth she hoped he'd accept.

But Bill had already figured out that he had the upper hand in the negotiations. Jayne had trained him too well. "Sorry, but no can do tonight, Jayne. And next Tuesday is iffy. The Magruder report, you know."

Jayne knew. All fledgling accountants filled out the tedious and much-loathed monthly Magruder report, biding their time until they could palm it off onto someone with less seniority.

"You're welcome to find somebody else to finish your session if that'll be a problem."

There was a gleam in Bill's eyes that Jayne didn't like. She drew a deep breath. "No, I'll teach tonight and research the raw data for the Magruder. This was short notice for you anyway."

"You're sure?"

Anything to get out of this class. "Definitely. I'll have the course materials on your desk by noon tomorrow." The little weasel.

Just knowing that tonight was the last time she'd have to struggle to compose herself in front of Garrett Charles was enough for Jayne to settle down and do some actual work. Her confidence restored, she planned to lecture on bookkeeping, her favorite subject. She'd give the most detailed, information-laden lecture in the history of Pace Waterman seminars. She'd leave Garrett Charles overwhelmed by her brilliance.

But when Jayne strode confidently into the conference room, Garrett was conspicuously absent.

Deflated, she waited as long as she could before reluctantly beginning her lecture. Her best subject and he was going to miss it. He'd forever remember her as the bumbling, frizzy-headed—though that was entirely Sylvia's fault—Pace Waterman accountant.

At seven-fifteen, Garrett slipped into the room. Or tried to. Dressed in a severe charcoal suit, with white shirt and dark tie, he looked utterly stunning. As one, the female students sighed audibly.

"Sorry I'm late," he murmured. "I had a prior engagement."

Jayne's hormones leaped at the word "engagement." *No! You can't have him!* they shouted. *We want him! We want him!* and she had to calm them down by telling them that engagement didn't mean approaching marriage in this sense.

Of course while she conversed with her hormones, she was staring at him again. And realizing this triggered the hyperventilation and sweaty palms with which she was becoming so regrettably familiar.

Nevertheless, she sucked in her stomach, wiped her palms, held her breath and launched into the fabulous bookkeeping lecture she'd prepared. "I recommend the double entry method of keeping track of your income and expenses. Here's why..."

"Sylvia, I was brilliant! Absolutely brilliant!" Jayne hugged herself the next morning, then snatched the chocolate doughnut out of Sylvia's hand and whirled around her office.

"You're always brilliant." Sylvia sat on Jayne's couch and peeled the plastic cover off her coffee cup. "That's why I hang around you. I keep hoping some of your smarts will rub off on me."

"But you don't understand." Jayne bit into and hurriedly swallowed some of the doughnut. "This time I was *brilliant* brilliant. You should have seen their faces. The class hung on every word. There wasn't a sound out of them, not even when I forgot the eight o'clock break."

"You talked for two solid hours?"

"Yes! I was fantastic." Jayne returned to her desk, opened her coffee and emptied it into her favorite thermal mug. "When they left, everybody was real quiet and thoughtful."

"Are you sure they were awake?"

Jayne frowned. "Of course. They were digesting everything I'd told them."

Sylvia picked the walnuts out of her whole wheat apple muffin and dropped them into the ashtray. "You think maybe you gave them too much to eat?"

"Hardly. I could have gone on for another two hours." Jayne sipped her coffee to keep from running over and whisking the ashtray out of Sylvia's reach.

"Then why aren't you?" Sylvia asked and bit into her muffin.

"Why aren't I what?" Jayne asked crossly. If Sylvia didn't like nuts, why did she always get the same muffin? Why not blueberry? Why leave nuts in Jayne's ashtray all the time?

"Teaching two more hours. Why'd you get Bill to finish your classes?"

"He's got to learn sometime."

Sylvia popped the last of her muffin into her mouth and brushed her hands together. Jayne could see little brown crumbs dotting the forest-green leather of the sofa.

"But why *this* time?" Sylvia stood. "Honestly, Jayne. Here, according to you, was a gorgeous man sitting right in your class and you didn't even invite him for coffee afterward."

"Oh, please. He wouldn't go for coffee with me."

"Did you ask?"

"No," Jayne mumbled and took a huge bite of her doughnut so she wouldn't have to discuss the matter with Sylvia anymore.

"And now, in a move guaranteed to squelch any possibility that you two could get together—" Jayne nearly choked "—you've quit the class." Sylvia left, shaking her head. "Anyway, I'm glad you're reconsidering my cousin Vincent. I understand he's filled out some."

Sylvia was wrong, wrong, wrong—and not just about reconsidering Vincent. Jayne had done the right thing. It was pointless to wish for what one couldn't have, wasn't it? Especially if the wishing was interfering with the pursuit of what one *could* obtain, which was, in Jayne's case, a measure of corporate and financial security. If she achieved success in the business world now, then when the young men of her generation decided it was time to settle down and look around for suitable life mates, there would be nice, solid Jayne and her little nest egg, ready to hatch.

At least that had been the plan until now. Jayne wasn't going to be passively waiting around anymore. She may not be Garrett Charles material, but he'd shaken up her life in a good way, she told herself. After all, wasn't she planning a cruise with Sylvia?

So, on Tuesday night, just about the time Garrett Charles was entering the conference room at Pace Waterman, Jayne, attired in her velour robe with the threadbare elbows, was parked in front of her television set while dining on her favorite feel-good meal—canned ravioli, M&M's and diet cola. She'd swathed her head in a towel while her hair soaked in a deep conditioner, which promised to counteract the effects of Sylvia's recent home perm. The movie playing on her video recorder was *How to Marry a Millionaire,* from which Jayne hoped to pick up tips, both financial and matrimonial.

She picked up neither, but after consuming the ravioli and the M&M's—and adding rum to her diet cola—didn't really care.

She cared the next morning, though. A lot. However, there was a bonus to falling asleep on the couch with her head soaking in conditioner. Her hair, which had resembled a pale brown dandelion, now lay in greasy kinks reminiscent of corkscrew pasta. Jayne felt this was an improvement.

But her face was too pale. Color. She needed color. Eventually she folded one of her scarves into a headband and tied her hair back. In the bathroom mirror, a bare face stared back at her. Jayne wasn't used to seeing that much of her face at one time. She pulled out a few wisps of bangs, though they didn't want to wisp anymore and began a desperate search for the pearl earrings that her grandparents had given her for graduation and she hadn't worn since. Why bother with earrings when her hair usually covered her ears?

Friday was not shaping up into the best of days. She had doubts about her appearance when she caught regulars on her Park & Ride bus giving her second looks. Or, it could be the sunglasses she wore, but didn't everyone notice how blindingly bright the lights were? Had all the lightbulbs been changed for ones with a higher wattage? What a waste of taxpayer dollars.

Hoping to clear her head, she forced herself to walk at a brisker pace from the Galleria stop to the Transco Tower. Entering the air-conditioned foyer, she realized she'd left her business pumps at her apartment and would either have to wear the battered rain pair she kept in her office, or her tennis shoes all day.

"Hey, Jaynie!" hooted the delivery courier when Jayne tried to sneak past the reception area. She detested the name Jaynie. "Ooh, look who tied one on last night!" He grinned.

Jayne didn't grin back, her attention caught by the expression on Beth, the receptionist's face. *Gad, I must look awful.* The scarf apparently wasn't providing the pick-me-up to her appearance that she'd hoped.

"Weeeell," said Bill when she slunk by his cubicle. "Still waters run deep."

Jayne ignored his crack. "How was class last night?"

"You mean the class I'm teaching so *your* evenings would be free?" Bill grinned wolfishly and leaned back in his chair.

Jayne stared him down, hoping he'd tip over.

"Not talking, are you?"

"Not unless it's about class."

"Okay. I wanted to talk to you about that, too." Bill straightened in an abrupt shift from obnoxious to businesslike. "Mr. Waterman says he's had six calls from people in the class wanting to sign accounting agreements with us. That's twenty-five percent of the enrollment. There've only been three classes—what did you do to them? And more important, can you teach me how to do it?"

The only explanation Jayne could think of was that the people in her class missed her and didn't want to continue the course without her. Personally gratifying, but that wasn't going to encourage Bill, was it? And she wanted him to continue teaching, didn't she? So she shrugged. "No secret. I just followed the curriculum."

Bill raised an eyebrow. "There were comments about bookkeeping being too complicated."

Jayne wished she hadn't been quite so considerate of his feelings. "Then they weren't paying attention," she mumbled and edged away from Bill's cubicle.

"When *I* tried to review bookkeeping to see where you'd left off, it appeared that you didn't leave off anywhere." He leaned back in his chair so his head stuck out of the cubicle. "Did you really cover the whole section in one night?"

"I was on a roll." Jayne escaped, feeling defensive. Treat people like they've got brains and see what happens. On the other hand, the company had six new accounts, so Mr. Waterman should be happy.

But...didn't any of those six people request Jayne as their accountant?

Feeling sorry for herself, she shut her office door and sank onto the small sofa she'd inherited from the office's previous occupant. Opening the cruise brochure, she stared at Garrett Charles and sighed. So handsome. So out of reach.

So get over him. Closing the book on that part of her life, Jayne put on her reading glasses, and got to work on the stupid Magruder report for Bill.

After half an hour, she threw the pen she'd been chewing at the computer monitor in disgust. Sloppy, sloppy, sloppy. No wonder Bill wanted to palm off the Magruder. Standards had really fallen since Jayne had paid her dues by filing the report. She'd hoped to finish it within an hour and get to her own work, but that wasn't going to be.

Examining back copies of the weekly report, Jayne discovered an error that had been repeated for at least three months. She didn't have time to go back further, but some poor intern would.

She was composing a memo to Mr. Waterman about the problem, when the silver-haired gentleman knocked on her open door.

'Jayne, are you busy?'' It was a rhetorical question and they both knew it.

"No," Jayne answered, just as rhetorically. At least she hoped Mr. Waterman knew she was speaking rhetorically.

"Good. I'd like you to meet a new client." He stood to one side and a tall, dark-haired man carrying a briefcase entered Jayne's office. "This is Garrett Charles. He's requested you to be his account executive."

CHAPTER THREE

AT FIRST, Garrett wasn't certain that the frozen woman who stared at him from behind a massive wooden desk was the same Jayne Nelson who'd taught the first two accounting sessions he'd attended. The glasses and the slicked-back hair momentarily threw him.

But the dazed look was one with which he was disagreeably familiar. Being a retired model and coming from a family of models, Garrett was well aware of his appearance and its effect on people.

Most women stared when they first encountered Garrett Charles. Since the time he'd become aware of girls and women—sometime after they'd become aware of him—Garrett had been the recipient of women's stares. Depending on the woman, eye contact might be anything from a quick assessing survey to stolen glances accompanied by giggles to frankly admiring gazes, which he preferred to the impersonally professional studies that were a part of his business. Rarely, however, was a woman in danger of going into shock the way Jayne Nelson was.

He'd assumed they were past the staring stage, but apparently not. Pale-faced, she hadn't blinked since Waterman had announced him. Assuming a pleasant expression, which he was prepared to hold until she recovered, Garrett advanced into the room.

"The Charles family incorporated some time ago

as Venus, Inc., a modeling firm. Their executive manager has resigned and the Charleses want Pace Waterman to take over as they expand the business.''

Jayne's eyes never left his face, Garrett noticed and doubted she'd even heard Waterman's summary of his situation.

He sighed inwardly. Years of training allowed him to keep his face in a bland mask until staring females realized what they were doing. Embarrassing them served no purpose except to make everyone feel uncomfortable. Unfortunately Jayne's boss didn't have the benefit of that training.

"Jayne?" A perplexed Waterman glanced from her shocked expression to Garrett and back again.

"Yes?" Her voice sounded thin and reedy.

"Are you quite well?"

Jayne blinked and her face and throat flamed in great patchy blotches. "Yes. I...was just concentrating. You caught me off guard." She made as if to push herself away from her desk and knocked a computer diskette to the floor. She ducked under the desk to retrieve it.

"Is now a bad time? I don't want to disturb you." Waterman was all solicitousness but Garrett knew he was really saying, "Get your act together, woman! An account with huge potential is on the line here!"

Jayne knew, too. Her face got even redder and Garrett battled disappointment. He'd hired Pace Waterman solely to work with Jayne. In spite of her rattled behavior around him, he enjoyed watching her as she tackled accounting, a subject she obviously liked, and wanted those in the class to like, too. He'd even enjoyed the other night when she'd gotten carried away and lectured right through the break. Imagine loving numbers that much. Unfortunately he hadn't been able to apply the lesson to his own books and had been irritated to discover that she'd no longer be teaching the class.

George Windom, Venus's longtime business and financial manager, had tendered his resignation and was gone before Garrett could hire a replacement. He'd hoped Jayne could be that replacement, but now, watching as she stood, he decided to request another accountant. A male. But not the one who was now teaching the class. Garrett was on the verge of suggesting he return at another time, when Waterman launched into an unnecessary introduction.

"Garrett, this is Jayne Nelson, one of our top accountants." Waterman may have added the last bit to remind himself as well as demonstrate his support of Jayne. "But, of course, you two have already met."

"Yes, yes, we have. Already met. He was in my class. Or the class that was mine, but currently is Bill's," Jayne babbled to Waterman, who was now looking at her with real apprehension.

Visibly steeling herself, Jayne turned her head and met Garrett's eyes, thrusting out her arm across the desk, presumably to shake his hand.

They never completed the ritual because Jayne knocked over her pencil holder scattering pencils, paper clips and pens over the surface of her desk.

"Oh—!"

Garrett couldn't hear what she said, but suspected it wasn't anything profane. Jayne didn't look like the swearing type.

Grabbing for the pens that rolled toward the edge,

Garrett deliberately knocked into her stacking file baskets, collapsing them on one corner and sending the files over the side.

Jayne sent him a stunned look—a different stunned look.

"I'm sorry. And here I was trying to help," he announced cheerfully, including Waterman in his smile.

Mr. Waterman's lips parted, but no sound emerged.

Jayne scrambled around her desk, banging her shin. Garrett winced at the sound.

"My, dear!" exclaimed Waterman ineffectually.

"I'm fine!" Jayne squeaked, grabbed her leg and hobbled a few steps before sinking to the floor at their feet.

Setting his briefcase well out of the way, Garrett stooped to help her gather the files.

"Let me help—"

"I'll just get these—"

They both reached for the same folder and their fingers brushed together.

Jayne jerked back as though she'd touched a live coal and quickly sprang to her feet—too quickly. On the way up, she banged her head on the desktop overhang.

Gasping, she rubbed her temple, smearing herself with blue ink and dislodging her glasses, which clattered to the desk.

A flabbergasted Waterman stared at her. "Jayne?"

"Are you all right?" Garrett asked.

Jayne stopped rubbing her head, leaving a patriotic red and blue against her white skin. "In spite of evidence to the contrary, I'm fine."

Garrett was caught by her naked brown eyes. He'd seen those eyes alight with her passion for numbers, sparkling when someone in the class would involuntarily exclaim, "Now I get it!" He also remembered her embarrassed sympathy when she bashed him with the cart. And of course the mesmerized stare with which she'd greeted his entrances to the conference room.

But he'd never seen her eyes dark with self-contempt the way they were now.

Garrett knew that if he asked for another accountant after what had just happened, Jayne would suffer, maybe even lose her job. After only a few minutes of conversation, Garrett knew Waterman was of the old school of businessmen who resisted the influx of women. Jayne probably was their best accountant, male or female. She'd have to be to have progressed as far as she had with the company.

And so Garrett smiled reassuringly at Jayne, earning a melted chocolate look in response. He turned to Waterman and offered his hand with more success than Jayne. "Thanks for your time, Mr. Waterman. I'd like to coordinate my calendar with Jayne's and then I'll stop by your office before I leave."

"Yes, *do* stop by." Waterman looked as though he didn't think it was a good idea to leave a new client with the self-destructive Ms. Nelson, but couldn't argue in the face of an obvious dismissal. To Jayne he said, "You have ink on your face."

Jayne mewled in distress, grabbed a tissue and rubbed at her temple, so Garrett followed Waterman to the door and closed it behind him.

With huge eyes, Jayne watched his progress back to where she stood in front of her desk.

Contemplating his next move—and he had no doubt the next move was up to him—Garrett stopped in front of her. Perhaps the direct approach would be best. "Ms. Nelson...Jayne, do I frighten you?"

"N-no." Jayne supposed it had been too much to hope that Garrett would ignore her peculiar behavior or attribute it to a momentary, and uncharacteristic, clumsiness. No, he had that darned book cart incident for reference. She fit the leg of the file basket back into the holder. At least he had his clumsy moments, too.

While she repaired her baskets, Garrett had stooped to gather the scattered files. "I don't frighten you?" he asked, standing and giving them to her.

"No." Jayne spoke more firmly this time. Fascinate, yes, frighten, no. She plopped the papers into the basket, determined to treat Garrett just as she would any other client.

Garrett studied her a moment then contorted his face and took a sudden step toward her.

Jayne yelped.

"Time for you to switch to decaf." He grinned.

"Why did you do that?" she demanded, her heart still racing.

"If you're going to be so jumpy, you ought to have a real reason."

"That's not a real reason," Jayne grumbled returning to her chair.

"Sure it is," he said cheerfully. "You never know when I'm going to do it again."

"You'd deliberately scare me again?"

"Maybe." He looked at her, flinched, and Jayne started. Garrett laughed. "And maybe not."

Jayne held her hand over her heart. "Okay, you've made your point." An unorthodox method, but surprisingly effective. Jayne presumed it was because her body had used its entire store of adrenaline during the past five minutes.

Garrett pulled over one of the tweed club chairs from the conversation area by the sofa. "Are you always this nervous, or just when you're around me?"

"Just around you," she admitted, surprising herself and apparently Garrett as well.

"Interesting." He leaned forward, his whole body folded attractively, as though he were posing for an advertisement. "Why is that?"

Jayne knew exactly why, but it didn't bode well for their future business relationship for her to tell him. "Well, you stare at me all the time!" Better to go on the attack. But perhaps a different attack would have been more effective.

"I...*stare* at you?" he asked, staring at her.

"Yes." *Weak, Jayne. Really weak.*

"I'll have to remember not to do that," he murmured, averting his eyes to look down at one manicured hand.

Or at least Jayne assumed it was manicured. She, herself, had never had a manicure. Too much bother. Besides, she was always snagging her cuticles when she searched through files. She curled her fingers in her lap and tried to deal with the fact that the epitome of masculine pulchritude was sitting on the other side of her desk.

"I was disappointed when you stopped teaching the class." He picked at a thread in the piping on the chair arm.

"You were?" He was?

Still avoiding her eyes, he nodded. "I'd always intended to hire an accountant and business manager to replace George, the man who resigned." Garrett glanced up, then back down quickly, making Jayne feel guilty for accusing him of staring. "I still can't believe he's gone. He was like a member of the family. Then, when he left so suddenly, I found myself trying to make sense of the firm's financial records."

The part of Jayne's brain that wasn't occupied with drooling over Garrett noted what he said and flagged it for further study.

"I've studied business and managerial accounting, but I must be rusty because I still can't figure out what George was doing." He gave her an endearingly sheepish smile.

"Oh, it's my fault," Jayne protested, responding to his dimples. "I shouldn't have given you so much to absorb during the second class."

Garrett shook his head. "You're a fine teacher."

"I am?" she breathed, losing herself in his gaze.

"Yes." He smiled and Jayne shivered.

"But," he continued, reaching into his breast pocket and removing an agenda, "I'd like to go over some points in your bookkeeping lecture again. I'm determined to thoroughly understand what's been going on at Venus before I turn over the records to anyone else."

Which was exactly why Jayne volunteered to teach the courses she did. People gave too much leeway to the business professionals they hired. She hated making decisions on behalf of clients who didn't understand the risks or the benefits of a particular action. She relaxed a bit. She and Garrett were going to get along just fine.

Of course, it would be best if they conducted most of their business over the phone so she wouldn't be distracted by his eyes and lips. And jaw and cheekbones. And the cleft in his—

"When would be a convenient time for us to meet?" He clicked a gold pen and waited.

Annnnytime. "Uh, now is fine. I'm not busy." Jayne punched the memo on the Magruder report into oblivion.

"You're sure?" At Jayne's nod, he returned the agenda and pen to his breast pocket and reached for his silver metal briefcase. "I brought Venus's most recent ledgers. Maybe if you used those as an example, I could figure out the rest of it myself."

"Okay." Jayne swiveled in her chair and grabbed her calculator. Usually, when a client brought files, Jayne would move to the sofa where they could spread everything out on the coffee table. But just before she mentioned moving, her eye caught the brochure with Garrett's picture inside. It was the only brochure on the table.

No need to panic. She'd simply move the brochure aside, preferably before he noticed. And even if he did notice it, there was no reason for him to suspect that she'd been mooning over his picture like a teenager with a celebrity tabloid.

"Why don't you bring the books over here where we can spread out," she suggested, hoping she could at least walk across the room without tripping. She ought to be able to, since she was still wearing her tennis shoes.

Garrett followed her to the leather sofa, which Jayne approached without incidence. She reached for the brochure.

"Going on a trip?" Garrett picked up the brochure before Jayne could. "My last modeling job is in here."

"Really?" Her voice sounded too high. She cleared her throat.

"Yeah, in the promos for the cruise line. I got a nice little trip to Mexico out of the shoot." He started to thumb through the brochure when it opened right to the page of the people lounging around the swimming pool.

Jayne wanted to disappear. Instead, her legs gave way and she sat on the sofa with a smack, listening in embarrassment as the air hissed out of the leather cushions.

The instant the magazine fell open to the pool picture, Garrett knew the brochure hadn't been on Jayne's office coffee table by chance. She was obviously embarrassed about being caught with it and wanted to pretend that she didn't know about his picture.

He didn't know why; he wouldn't have minded her commenting. But for her sake, he'd pretend nothing was out of the ordinary. In fact, maybe if he deglamorized modeling to her, she wouldn't feel so in awe of him. He sat on the sofa next to her, feeling her tense, and spread the advertisement open. "It was freezing outside when we took this shot. In fact it was so cold, we had to hold our breaths so there wouldn't be little white clouds in the photographs.''

"You did?"

Garrett nodded and pointed to dock buildings in the background. "Computer retouching got rid of the Christmas decorations.''

"But you're in swim trunks. Weren't you cold?''

"Yes, but it was supposed to be fun in the sun, so we had to look like we were having fun.'' He smiled. "It's worse to model winter wear in the heat, though.''

"Why don't you stick with the right seasons?''

"Magazine lead times run months in advance. Ad campaigns start even before that. We shoot Christmas in July and Father's Day at Christmas.'' He closed the brochure and set it aside. "But thank God I'm out of that end of the business now.''

Jayne's eyes widened. "Didn't you like being a model?''

He'd hated being a model, but in his family there was nothing else. He'd grown up in a world in which he'd been judged by the smallest details of his appearance. The right look guaranteed prosperity. The wrong look meant unemployment. Photographers and advertisers cared only about the way he and the other members of his family looked, not who they were. They were merely props used to sell a product.

It had taken him six years to extricate himself. Six years to convince his family that he could run and expand the agency. And now he was going to have to trust the business acumen of the young woman sitting next to him. She deserved an honest answer to her question. "No," he said quietly. "I didn't enjoy being a model."

"Why not?"

Their thighs were touching. Jayne wondered if Garrett noticed. She noticed. She was afraid to breathe in case the slight movement made him shift away from her. If only there were more nerve endings in thighs. Even the nerve endings in other parts of her body were petitioning to become thigh nerves.

And she and Garrett were talking. Together. An actual conversation where Jayne asked pertinent questions. Not profound questions, but she wasn't gaping at him or knocking something over. In another few minutes, he might realize she had a brain. She hoped he liked brains.

It's not your brain you want him interested in.

Where had that hideous, but regrettably correct thought come from? She'd been hanging around Sylvia too much.

"Modeling isn't the glamorous profession everyone believes it is." He smiled a brief, perfect smile and turned to the records he'd brought. "Remind me and I'll tell you all about it sometime."

Oh, right. Back to work. He was paying for her expertise, not to have her make goo-goo eyes at him. Annoyed with the unprofessional direction of her thoughts, she scooted a couple of inches away from him and tried to focus on the ledgers. She'd ask about his computer equipment and backups later. "This seems fairly straightforward...where have you been having difficulties?"

Garrett leaned over to point to a column of figures bringing his face to within inches of hers, but Jayne, after an initial jolt, managed to concentrate on what he was saying. "This is our gross income."

"Yes."

He flipped to the next section. "These columns tell where it went. Therefore, when I add all the expenses columns together, it should equal the income, right?"

"Not necessarily," Jayne began. "It appears your former accountant was escrowing a percentage..." She set her calculator on the table and jabbed in some numbers. "Twenty-seven percent here...thirty-three percent on this deposit, probably for taxes."

"I know. But I added that into expenses and compared it with receipts...or tried to. The total amount never completely agreed with the bank statements."

Jayne leveled a look at him. "It either agrees or it doesn't. Incomplete agreement isn't a choice."

He looked as though he wanted to argue the point, but didn't. "Then the numbers don't agree."

"So we'll make them agree or find out why they don't." Jayne spoke with complete confidence. This was her turf and one she knew well. "Perhaps there's been a simple math error, or numbers have been transposed. But since your former accountant knew he was leaving the books for someone else to take over, I would expect him to reconcile all accounts prior to his departure, making math errors unlikely."

Garrett's expression tightened. "You're saying it's *my* fault I can't understand these numbers? That they're *beyond* me?"

"Of course not." Jayne was surprised at his tone. She'd obviously hit a sore point with him. "I'm merely posing possible explanations and ranking them in order of probability. Under these circumstances, a math error is least probable. Therefore, we should focus our efforts on a more likely reason for the discrepancy.''

He weighed her words, taking several moments before nodding. ''Sorry I jumped on you. George—Windom, the man you're replacing—George never wanted to explain the business side of Venus to me. Told me it wasn't necessary for me to know. Maybe he didn't think I could grasp the complexities of his job.'' Garrett's words held a subtle challenge. ''Unfortunately, in my line of work, I've run into too many people who doubt my mental capabilities.''

Jayne's brow furrowed. ''Why?''

Garrett blinked at her, then a slow smile spread over his face lighting his eyes with an emotion Jayne couldn't read. She could see his gaze dart over her face, as though he was acquainting himself with details of her appearance he hadn't bothered to notice before now. ''How do you propose to solve the discrepancy problems?'' he asked after a moment.

Feeling unsettled, Jayne was glad to have something to say. ''By first making certain we understand the method your accountant used.''

''Very diplomatically put.''

He never answered her question, but Jayne sensed that something had changed between them. As she reviewed bookkeeping procedures with Garrett, she noticed that he was looking at her in a different way. A layer between them had been removed and she'd never even known it was there.

''It's obvious you understand accounting procedures,'' Jayne said after their discussion. ''Now put that understanding into practice. I suggest that you take Mr. Windom's final report and try to re-create it."

"He didn't leave a final report."

"What?" This did not bode well for the state of the books.

"He just—" Garrett spread his hands "—left."

"Without..." Jayne belatedly registered the underlying hurt she heard in his voice. "And he'd been with you how many years?"

"Ever since my parents resumed full-time modeling when I was fourteen. So...sixteen years."

"Your *parents* modeled?" Jayne asked as she calculated his age.

Garrett nodded. "Still do. And my sister and brother, Sasha and Sandor. They're twins. You may have noticed them in ads lately?"

Jayne shook her head. She wasn't much for fashion magazines.

"They really do look a lot alike and they've played that into a nice career."

"Do they look like you?"

He lifted a shoulder. "There's a family resemblance. Anyway, they filmed several commercials when they were younger, but when they hit thirteen and grew about two feet overnight, their modeling careers took off. They're more successful than my parents and me put together. And *that's* when we incorporated. It was cheaper to hire one full-time booking agent for all of us than pay commissions to another agency."

He must have had a very interesting childhood. One about as different from Jayne's quiet, middle-class, only-child background as could be. "I don't suppose you ever conducted an outside audit of your books?''

Garrett shook his head before she finished speaking.

Of course they wouldn't have asked for an audit, she thought. From what Garrett had told her, this George Windom had been practically one of the family. It wouldn't have occurred to them to suggest an audit. But it should have occurred to their manager. He was in a position of enormous trust—and enormous responsibility. An outside audit would have protected both parties. Even so, there was absolutely no excuse for the man leaving without a final reconciliation. ''I apologize on behalf of my profession.'' There didn't seem to be anything else she could say.

''Don't blame George,'' Garrett said. ''I turned down all the bookings he'd made after the cruise job. I'd told him I was quitting, but he obviously didn't believe me. But I had plans for the company and he must have resented having one of us in the office calling the shots after so many years.''

''Maybe he thought you didn't need him anymore.''

''Of course we needed him. I can't run the entire operation by myself.'' Garrett stacked the ledgers into his briefcase. ''George never gave me a chance to discuss his role in the company with him. Three weeks ago, I walked into my office and found his letter on my desk. His home phone had been disconnected. I don't even know where to send his final paycheck.''

Jayne skipped asking about family or relatives who might know Mr. Windom's whereabouts. It wasn't any of her business. However, the state of the books was. "Garrett, this all sounds very ominous."

"No, no." He shook his head. "I know where you're going and you're wrong. I think George is trying to show us how much we need him. He'll be gone just long enough for things to get in a real mess, then come riding in to the rescue."

Jayne tapped the briefcase. "Things are in a mess now. You can't make the books balance. And if you can't..." She drew in a breath. "Well, I don't have a magic calculator."

Garrett stood. "I'm going to give it another try. But whether he returns or not, I still want you to be Venus's accountant and bookkeeper." As he spoke, he offered a hand to Jayne, which she took, impressed by the small courtesy. "George will act strictly as a booking agent. Since we're signing on more models, he'll have plenty to do." With a squeeze, he released her hand.

At that moment, a foot pushed open the door. "Jayne, it was your turn to get coffee. But since you're always working so hard and since I'm such a *wonderful* friend, I—" Sylvia got that far before she spotted Garrett.

Jayne watched her go slack-jawed as she stood stock-still, a cup of coffee and a white paper bag in each hand.

Beside Jayne, Garrett, too, had gone still, his face arranged in a polite smile. As the seconds passed, Jayne's gaze darted from Garrett to Sylvia and back to Garrett again, watching for his reaction. It was as though time stopped until Sylvia blinked.

"I'm so sorry. I didn't realize you were busy."

Nevertheless, she advanced into Jayne's office, her eyes on Garrett.

"I was just leaving," Garrett murmured.

"So soon?" Sylvia gave an artificial little laugh that made Jayne's eyes widen in horror. "We've only just met." Her gaze flicked to Jayne. "Or were about to."

Jayne's tongue stuck to the roof of her mouth. "Garrett Charles, this is Sylvia Dennison, a friend of mine. Garrett is my *client,* Sylvia," Jayne added with a look her friend missed, since she was busy telegraphing "I'm available" to Garrett.

"Coffee?" Sylvia oozed forward and offered him one of the cups she held. Probably Jayne's.

Garrett swiftly checked his watch. "It'll have to be some other time."

"When?" Sylvia gazed up at him.

"Sometime when I'm not on my way to another appointment." Garrett smiled briefly, then turned to Jayne. "I'll call you after I go over the books again."

This time, his smile was warm and bracketed by dimples.

She heard Sylvia sigh.

"Let me know when you're ready for me to take over," Jayne said and walked him to the door.

"I'll do that. Thanks, Jayne." Another dazzling smile and he was gone.

Jayne took her time shutting the door so she could watch his progress down the hall.

"Oh...my...God." With a squeal, Sylvia collapsed onto the sofa. "Ohmygod, ohmygod." She fanned herself with her hand. "He's *gorgeous!* How can you *stand* being near him and not ripping off all your clothes and screaming 'take me now'?''

"I *have* been having a little problem with that,' Jayne murmured, but Sylvia wasn't listening.

"Look at me." She held out her hand. "I'm shaking. *Shaking.*"

Jayne was torn between relief to know she wasn't alone in her reactions to Garrett and envy that Sylvia felt so free to express hers. And express she did.

"He's the one, Jayne."

"Mr. Right?"

"No, silly. The man to make me forget everything. I want to live with him in a dirty garret in a foreign country. I want to exist on bread, wine, cheese and hours of meaningless sex." She closed her eyes on a sigh. "I want to be his love slave."

Except for the dirty garret part, it all sounded appealing to Jayne.

Sylvia bolted upright. "Do you think he liked me?"

I hope not.

"When he said 'sometime when I'm not on my way to another appointment,' was he *sincere?* Or was he just giving me the brush-off?"

"I think he was just being polite."

"No." Sylvia shook her head. "He was *looking* at me." She tapped her chest.

"Because you were standing two inches away from him."

"I…" Sylvia's mouth opened and closed. She narrowed her eyes. "You're jealous."

"I am not!"

But she was. How absurd. There was not even a

remote chance that plain Jayne Nelson would ever be Garrett Charles's love slave.

"I didn't think you were interested in him. If you want him for yourself, say the word and I'll back off."

Good old Sylvia, actually thinking Jayne had a chance. "No...he's all yours."

Sylvia dived into her white bag and withdrew her usual muffin. "Promise me that if he calls, you'll give him my number."

"Sylvia, I think he's got your number already."

"Promise!"

"Okay, okay."

"I mean, it's not as though I haven't tried to fix *you* up with anybody," she said and began picking out the nuts. "Vincent is trying to get extra time off so he can take you out."

"I don't want to go out with your second cousin."

"Sure you do—we can double date. You and Vincent and me and Garrett."

Jayne sighed.

By the time Sylvia left, Jayne was feeling decidedly cranky. She finished composing her memo on the errors in the Magruder report, e-mailed a copy to Bill, and concentrated fiercely on the rest of her work so that she'd be free should Garrett call. She didn't expect him to, but with Sylvia the barracuda after him, she felt she ought to do something.

She just didn't know what or how.

It was late afternoon when her phone buzzed and she answered it to hear Garrett's molten voice on the line.

"Jayne, I've got a problem," he said immediately after identifying himself.

"You found the reason for the discrepancy in your books?"

He made a harsh sound. "No...I found that all the checks I've written on the agency account have bounced."

CHAPTER FOUR

JAYNE had been nearly as surprised as Garrett had been. She distinctly remembered that the final bank statement had reported a healthy balance. Garrett had kept the checkbook up-to-date. There was still a healthy balance.

Except that when Jayne contacted the bank vice president, Elaine, with whom she'd worked previously, the woman readily confirmed the figures. Two weeks ago, the Venus, Inc. business manager had withdrawn nearly all the liquid assets.

"But George Windom resigned three weeks ago," Jayne protested.

Through the phone there was the sound of computer keys tapping. "We were not informed that he should no longer have access to the accounts," Elaine told her.

Of course they hadn't been. Garrett hadn't accepted Windom's resignation. He thought he would be coming back.

So. George Windom had waited a week, then cleaned them out. The action was premeditated, Jayne knew. He'd waited until the bank statements had been closed for the month so he'd have the maximum amount of time before what he'd done could be discovered.

And Jayne was going to have to tell Garrett. Not

only that, she suspected—no, sadly, she *knew*—worse discoveries were to come.

They agreed that Jayne would come to the agency the next morning and conduct a complete audit of the books.

She was so concerned about how Garrett would react to the news of his manager's betrayal, that she barely gave a thought to her own appearance.

Other than washing her hair three times to remove the excess conditioner.

And changing her outfit twice. There was a fine line between inspiring confidence and intimidating. She wanted Garrett and his family to feel reassured, even though privately, Jayne didn't think she'd find much to reassure them about.

Thus, she wore her ''breaking-bad-news'' outfit. It was identical to her inspiring confidence suit, but the look was softened with a pale blue blouse and pastel-striped ascot.

Venus, Inc. was not located in the Galleria mall, after all, but across busy Westheimer on Post Oak, smack in the middle of Pavilion, an area featuring exclusive designer boutiques catering to Houston's wealthy elite.

Jayne had seen the amount of rent they were paying and was expecting a larger place than the one she found wedged between an antique shop and a stationers.

Black marble surrounded glass doors with brass handles. Very classy, she thought approvingly and pushed them open.

Jayne felt as though she'd stepped into a different world, or at least had been transported to another planet. The women waiting in the starkly pale gray reception area looked like no human beings she knew. Images bombarded her, primarily, bones, skin, legs and lips.

The women were young, tall and impossibly thin. They weren't pretty—at least the kind of pretty Jayne wanted to be, but the giant pictures covering the walls made them, or women like them, look gorgeous and stunning and alluring and sophisticated and other things Jayne knew she'd never be.

And then she saw them—photos of what must be the entire Charles family beneath the curving script of the Venus, Inc. logo. There were five pictures displayed together, including one of a younger Garrett in a black leather jacket, which he wore open without a shirt underneath.

Mesmerized, Jayne took three steps toward it before making eye contact with a young woman behind the desk.

"May I help you?" the receptionist asked.

She wore her dark hair short and spiky, in the kind of cut that would send Jayne screaming from the hairdresser, or from Sylvia who would have probably been the one to talk her into it.

"I'm Jayne Nelson. Would you please tell Garrett that I'm here?"

The receptionist ran a bony finger down a scheduling book. "Did you have—"

"I'm an accountant," Jayne interrupted, so anyone within earshot wouldn't think she was here to audition as a model—not that they would.

"So he's expecting you?" The young woman paused with her hand on the intercom.

Jayne nodded, pleased that the receptionist hadn't made some denigrating crack.

Within seconds after the receptionist notified him, Garrett appeared in the far doorway and beckoned to her. "I am *very* glad to see you," he said and exhaled with a smile that revealed both dimples and white teeth. "We're still setting up and will be with you all in a minute," he called to the room at large, then turned his blue, blue eyes to Jayne again.

Jayne's heart picked up the pace a little, even though she knew he was just relieved that she was here to help with the financial crisis and not thrilled to see her again because he was bowled over with desire for her.

He led her down a hallway, adorned with more black-and-white blowups of models. She looked for another picture of him, but didn't find one.

"I've put you in George's office," Garrett said and gestured her into a room that was generously proportioned, considering the overall space occupied by the agency.

Feet sinking into marshmallow-soft carpeting, Jayne approached the desk, running her finger across the smooth wooden surface as she walked around to the leather executive chair. The furnishings looked solid, dark and expensive, clashing with the contemporary appearance of the reception area, not that the reception area looked cheap, or anything, but George obviously had been given a free rein in decorating his office space.

"All the agency financial records are in the files, here." Garrett waved an arm toward two wooden filing cabinets that matched the desk. "Feel free to look through anything you want. If you need something and can't find me, ask Micky, the receptionist, though I'd appreciate it if you could keep the reason you're here between us, for now.''

"Sure."

He smiled at her again and this time, Jayne noticed the strain that pulled at the edges. Considering everything, he was holding up remarkably well, but Jayne wished she could say something to reassure him, something like, "This is all just a computer glitch and I'll have it straightened out in no time."

But she couldn't and he was too smart to believe her if she did. "I have to tell you that the bulk of the money in the agency account was withdrawn in a lump sum two weeks ago." Might as well get the bad news over right away.

"George?" he asked.

Jayne nodded, not adding any of her suspicions. "The bank is tracing it. In the meantime, I'm going to get right to work so I can tell you what's happened with the books as quickly as I can."

"Thanks." Garrett gazed at the impressionist painting that hung over the filing cabinets. Jayne suspected that it was an original.

"I transferred money from my own checking account to cover the outstanding agency checks." He glanced at her. "Or those of which I'm aware."

"When I spoke with the bank yesterday, I told them not to honor any checks written by George Windom. You'll have to fill out new signature cards to make it official, though."

"Right."

"Garrett?"

He turned to her.

"I wouldn't wait too long."

He gave a curt nod. "I'll get to the bank sometime today." He moved toward the door. "As you saw, I've got a roomful of hopeful models. Thursday is our weekly open house."

"Garrett, go now," Jayne urged firmly before he could leave. "Ask to speak with Elaine Ormand."

Their eyes met and a flash of pain shot through his.

"Okay," he agreed and was gone.

Jayne made a little sound of distress. Poor Garrett. He'd been betrayed by a man who was a father figure to him. They'd all been betrayed, but Garrett was suffering the most, mainly because the others didn't know. He was a tragic figure and she, Jayne, had to help him. Even now, his handsome brow was probably furrowed in anguish, she thought with a romantic sigh.

But it had better be furrowed as he drove to the bank, the practical part of Jayne thought as she turned on the computer. In fact, before she delved deeply into the books, she ought to pop out and check to see if Garrett had left yet. On the basis of Jayne's word, Elaine had flagged the Venus account for her personal attention, but Jayne's word was only good until the end of business today. She wasn't entirely certain that Garrett understood this.

Jayne peered into the reception area, but didn't see him. Twice as many girls crowded the room as there had been before, but no Garrett.

"If you're looking for Garrett, he's in the studio." Micky, the receptionist, cheerfully slid off the stool and directed Jayne down the hall to a door at the end.

Jayne smiled her thanks, thinking that Micky was nice. She'd forgive her for the fact that she was so thin and tall that bad hair looked good on her.

The agency office space was thin and long, just like a model, Jayne thought as she walked toward the studio. Before she got to the end of the hall, a side door opened and a girl wearing a kimono and carrying a binder stepped out. She smiled nervously at Jayne and opened the door to the studio. Jayne followed her in and found herself at the end of a line of women waiting to speak to an older, chicly dressed woman.

"I'm sorry, but our minimum height requirement is five feet, eight inches." She smiled with professional sympathy and returned a form to a disappointed girl.

There was a flash and Jayne's attention was drawn to the other end of the room where a gray, wrinkled canvas backdrop hung from the ceiling. A photographer took pictures of swimsuit-clad girls. Beside him was Garrett, enjoying the view.

Or that's the way it appeared to Jayne. At any rate, he wasn't furrowing his brow, he didn't appear to be suffering, and there was nothing tragic about the way he was encouraging a brunette with a shy, full-lipped smile.

The girl relaxed, shifting her position. The camera flashed, and Garrett grinned at her. "That was great!" After he helped her on with her wrap, she showed him a book of pictures she'd brought.

So much for suffering the agonies of betrayal, Jayne thought, feeling foolish. But if he didn't get over to the bank, he'd be suffering the agonies of bankruptcy.

She'd warned him, given him her best professional advice. And professional was the key word here, she lectured herself as she left the studio without speaking to him. That was the only kind of relationship she was ever going to have with him.

Yes, she'd allowed herself to develop a silly crush on a client and no, that wasn't professional. At least she'd recognized how hopeless it was before she made a fool of herself.

Garrett Charles spent his days surrounded by beautiful women. He wasn't going to notice her. Not that way, at least.

Jayne would have to be satisfied with Garrett's gratitude after she discovered what George Windom had done and how he'd done it.

There was always the "shooting the messenger" danger, but she buried that thought. Sitting at the desk, she reached for the hardbound ledgers Garrett had brought to her office yesterday and looked forward to having that fabulous Garrett smile directed her way.

Three frustrating hours passed. Jayne was aware that they'd passed solely because Micky came to the door and offered to order lunch for her.

Jayne absently mumbled her agreement and it seemed like just a few seconds later that she looked up to find Garrett carrying two plastic domed plates and a couple of bottles of mineral water across the room. "Ready for a break?" he asked, setting the bottles on her desk. "I wouldn't have disturbed you, but you've been at it a long time."

She *had* been at it a long time, and frankly, she needed more to look forward to than Garrett's smile, fabulous though it was. Lunch would be an excellent start.

Suddenly hungry, Jayne turned off the computer monitor and stood, stretching out the kinks in her muscles. "Did you go to the bank?"

"Yes, ma'am," he said, making Jayne feel like a nag.

"I've had clients ignore my advice in the past and it caused problems," she explained.

He grimaced. "You gave an order, not advice."

"I'm sor—"

"No, you were right to insist. I would have put it off because once I change the bank cards, it means George is really gone."

If you're lucky, Jayne thought.

Garrett offered her a plate and a packet of plastic flatware. "So what's the story here? Bad news? Good news? No news?"

"No news." Jayne pried the dome off the plate and stared at a naked grilled chicken breast and fruit salad. A *small* naked grilled chicken breast.

"No news is good news?" Garrett had pulled a chair next to the desk and was already eating his lunch. He had the same thing in the same quantity she did.

"Not in this case." Jayne hated to sound discouraging, but the more she studied the records, the grimmer the situation became. "I am going to make some phone calls this afternoon. By the end of the day, I hope I can tell you where you stand." Jayne took a bite of the chicken. It tasted healthy, but it could use a smidgen of gravy. No, it needed a *lot* of gravy. Why couldn't gravy be healthy?

Garrett gestured toward the books and files that covered the desk, the credenza and the floor in between. "Could you give me a more detailed update?" He sounded casual, but Jayne knew he wasn't.

It was only natural that he was worried. The thing was, she didn't want to say anything yet because there was more than one explanation for why the totals didn't add up.

"I'd rather not," she said. "I'll just give you the bottom line when I find it." And she had a feeling that would be bad enough.

"I want to know how you reach the bottom line," he said with an edge to his voice. "If you'll explain the process, I'll try to keep up."

Try to keep up? Did he think she doubted that he could understand what happened? How absurd. "*I* can't even keep up!" Ripping off her glasses, she rubbed her temples. "Every time I think I've finally figured out what Windom has done, I haven't." She met Garrett's eyes. "I wanted to have the answers for you right away, but it's just a huge, giant mess!"

To her horror, she felt her eyes burn, which meant tears were on the way. Sure she was way overdue for a break, but now she was about to be hideously unprofessional. It was just that she had wanted to appear to be brilliantly clever because brains was all she had and she wanted Garrett to admire her for *something*.

She rubbed her forehead, hoping Garrett wouldn't notice her eyes.

He stood and a moment later, she felt his hand on her shoulder. He'd noticed. "I'm sorry I jumped on you. I...don't want you to keep anything from me.

It's not a matter of trust, it's that I need to understand what's going on.''

The weight of his hand was warm and reassuring. Jayne thought being taken into his arms and being held close to his chest would be even more warm and reassuring, but Garrett squeezed her shoulder then withdrew his hand.

"It's okay." Jayne swallowed and blinked back the tears before her eyes could fill. "I'm still lost, myself, right now and need more information."

"Is there any way I can help?" Garrett asked.

Jayne thought of the phone calls to be made. Garrett could make the calls. In fact, it would be best if he did. "Sure, if you've got the time."

"I've made time." He snapped the cover back on his half-eaten lunch. "Tomorrow is Friday. Payday."

"And there's nothing in the checking account."

"Nope."

Jayne lost her appetite, a first for her. She snapped the cover back on her own lunch and set it aside. "You'll have to liquidate some of your investments."

"What's the penalty for cashing in a CD early?" he asked.

Jayne brightened. "You've got CDs? Where?"

"Aren't they listed in the books?"

Uh-oh. Jayne shook her head, the few bites of chicken she'd eaten sitting heavily in all its low-fat splendor in her stomach.

Garrett strode over to the file cabinets and yanked open a drawer. Jayne hoped he'd find something. But having combed through the files earlier, she knew he wouldn't.

And he didn't.

"There *were* CDs," Jayne said. "The last of them was cashed in three years ago."

"Cashed in?" Garrett looked stunned. "Why? Does it say?"

Jayne pointed to one of the ledgers. "It appears Windom was investing. You own shares in several limited partnerships." Which looked suspicious to her, but she said nothing.

"I don't remember any of this."

"Could he have told your parents?"

"Possibly." Garrett walked around the desk to stand beside her and stare at the ledgers. "They would have agreed to anything he recommended. That was George's job. They couldn't keep up with business details. We were all booked heavily during that time, flying from one shoot to another." He gave a short humorless laugh. "I think we actually went an entire year without all being in the same place at the same time. But the jobs were there and when I wasn't in school, I was working." He shook his head, no doubt blaming himself.

Great, Jayne. You've depressed the client. "Hey, let's don't panic until we see what the investments are worth. That's what I'd planned to do this afternoon." Jayne handed him the stack of files she'd pulled. "These are statements and transaction verifications. They should have phone numbers somewhere on them."

"And what information do you want?"

"Current value and liquidation procedures."

Slowly Garrett took the files. "Do you mind if I work in here?"

Mind? Mind having Garrett in the same room with

her for an entire afternoon? Was he kidding? "Sure! I mean, no, I don't mind."

When he saw Jayne's face light up, Garrett almost changed his mind. He wasn't going to be as much help as she obviously expected. Though he was trying to hide it, from himself as well as from the Venus staff, Garrett was worried. He also didn't want to chance being overheard, which was the main reason he wanted to make the calls from this office.

Too, he found being around Jayne comforting. For a moment, he'd thought she was patronizing him, but quickly realized his mistake. She'd been working with an incredible intensity the past several hours. He'd looked in on her when he'd returned from the bank, and she'd never noticed.

Yeah, if he had to have a financial crisis, Jayne Nelson was the person to have it with.

Clearing a spot at the edge of the desk, Garrett moved the telephone and made his first call.

The number had been disconnected.

Jayne stopped what she was doing and searched the files for the most recent statement from M&I Energy Partnership, Limited, but it appeared the one Garrett had, dated the previous August, *was* the most recent.

"I don't see a tax statement from them for last year." She flipped through the agency tax return. "M&I *is* listed as an asset here."

"How about the year before?" Garrett noticed that she'd gone through at least five years' worth of returns.

"It's here as well." She was silent a moment as she compared the two returns.

Yeah, if anyone could get him out of this mess, Jayne could do it. Garrett watched her concentrate. Her head moved just enough to bounce one of her curls against her cheek, drawing his attention. She had great skin, a creamy white most models would envy.

He was surprised by an impulse to touch it, maybe to tuck the curl behind her ear.

Jayne beat him to it, looking up and shoving her hair out of the way. "Same figures."

"What does that mean?"

"Well, it could—"

"Jayne."

She reluctantly met his eyes and Garrett's stomach knotted. "What does that mean?" he repeated.

"It means that M&I had two identical operating years in a row, down to the penny, or that George Windom fabricated the numbers."

Garrett stared at the now worthless piece of paper in the file. With a sudden, savage movement, he crumpled it and threw it at the trash can where it bounced off the rim and rolled across the floor. Even with all the evidence to the contrary, he still hadn't wanted to believe that George had stolen from them.

"I can check on the Internet—"

"Don't bother. You won't find this company or the money." Garrett closed the file and prepared to call the next name on his list, not that he held out much hope.

The same thing, or a variation happened with every other investment. George Windom had inflated values and invested poorly, then tried to cover his mistakes. He'd apparently been doing so for several years.

The bottom line was that the Charles family was, for all practical purposes, flat broke.

At the end of the afternoon, Garrett stared at the financial wreckage of his family's company. "Now I know why George ran," he said. "He knew with me working in the office I'd eventually figure out what he'd been doing. But did he have to clean us out?"

"He probably needed money to live on," Jayne offered in a small voice.

"But what are *we* supposed to live on?"

She shook her head, not that Garrett had expected her to have any answers.

He jabbed a finger at one of the ledgers. "Do you realize that George never deposited the last month's models' fees in escrow? He put the money in the checking account with the agency operating funds, which not only is *very* illegal, it means he stole from every model we represent. And when we don't pay them tomorrow, everyone in the industry will know it. Other agencies will snap them up and that's the end of Venus."

"Maybe not."

In spite of himself, Garrett felt a flicker of hope. "What do you mean?"

"I have a plan."

"You do?"

Coloring, she looked down. "Okay, not a complete plan. At least not yet."

"Oh, great."

At his disparaging tone, her head snapped up. "But I will! I just have to work out a few details."

He gazed into sincere, honest brown eyes, free of artifice. They demanded that he believe in her.

And so help him, he did. He sat back in the chair. "Okay, then. Let's talk details."

CHAPTER FIVE

A PLAN? Details? She had no plan. No details.

Jayne had no plan for Garrett because the only logical plan in this instance would be to file for bankruptcy right after calling the police and that's what she should have advised him. But she hadn't.

And why? Because of a noble desire to erase the anguish from his face? Ease the clenching of his jaw? Soothe away the pain of betrayal in his eyes?

Well, it was desire, all right, but it was the memory of his bare chest in the cruise brochure that compelled Jayne to try to find a way to continue working with Garrett.

If Garrett filed for bankruptcy, the lawyers would take over and Jayne would be out of the picture. She'd never see him again. Therefore, she'd offered a plan. A plan she did not yet have.

She was not proud of herself.

And now he sat there, expecting her to come up with something brilliant. She was an accountant, not a miracle worker.

But she *was* highly motivated.

"You do want to save your company?" she asked to verify that they were on the same wavelength.

"Of course!"

A belated sense of professionalism made her caution him. "It will be expensive."

"I never had any doubt," he said dryly.

"All right then." Jayne's last wisps of guilt evaporated. "Your top priority is to meet your financial obligations tomorrow. Can you do that out of your personal funds?"

Garrett shook his head. "Hardly. I tapped into them already."

"So we need another source." It was a measure of Jayne's desperation that she mentally checked her *own* bank balance. "What about your family?"

"I don't know. George handled our personal investments, too."

And no telling what he'd done with them, but that was a problem for another day. "Did he have access to your family's checking accounts?"

"I don't know."

"If they could, would they be willing to kick in to cover the payroll?"

Garrett drew a deep breath. "I don't know," he said once again.

"Can you find out?" Jayne asked, trying not to sound irritated. Here she was, actually coming up with a plan, and Garrett wasn't helping.

"They're in New York shooting Christmas catalogs. I'll leave a message for them at the apartment." He reached for the telephone.

"Garrett?" Jayne looked over at the landscape above the filing cabinets. "What's the painting worth?"

He followed her gaze. "Monetary value, or sentimental value?"

Jayne didn't answer.

"Sorry." Garrett waved away his question. "We

gave that to George last year on his fifteenth anniversary with us."

And all the time the man had been ripping them off. However, Jayne had learned that it was best to keep emotions out of financial discussions. "So, technically, you don't own it."

"I know where you're going with this." Garrett stared at the painting. "Tell you what. Let's leave that for our backup plan."

Backup plan? He was giving her too much credit. With a last glance at the painting, Jayne turned away from it. "Okay, but let's hope your family comes through."

Garrett nodded and picked up the phone.

During the next week, Jayne sometimes thought she *was* a miracle worker.

The payroll had been met only because Sasha and Sandor had foolishly, but fortunately, kept obscene balances in their checking accounts. Garrett's parents had "responsibly" stashed their earnings with George Windom, who presumably still had them.

After the payroll hurdle had been passed, Jayne had spent an idyllic weekend holed up in the office with Garrett going over the books in order to complete the audit. The going over the books part wasn't idyllic, but being with Garrett was. They sat side by side, arm to arm, calculator to calculator.

Numbers and Garrett—could it get any better?

He brought her food, more healthy grilled and steamed stuff, but she appreciated the thought. He even insisted that she take breaks and walked around the shops in the Pavilion courtyard with her. She expected a tour of the designer boutiques with a critique of the clothes in the windows, but the only window Garrett stopped in front of was the skiing display of a sporting goods store.

"Do you ski?" he asked.

Jayne instantly visualized herself in front of a cozy lodge fire with Garrett, but in truth hadn't been nearer to a snowflake than the instantly melting bits that occasionally tantalized Houston. "No," she said. "I'm more of a cruise person." Not that she and Sylvia had made any progress with their vacation plans.

"You ought to give skiing a try." He smiled down at her. "You'd like it."

There wasn't a hint of an invitation in his voice, and truthfully, Jayne hadn't expected one.

But a girl could dream, couldn't she?

The first time they went walking, she pretended that she and Garrett were an ordinary couple out for an afternoon, but every female they encountered underscored just how unordinary Garrett was.

Women stared. They weren't even subtle about it. Garrett didn't seem to notice, but Jayne did. She also noticed the curious glances she drew. The women were wondering what a mousy brown accountant was doing with Garrett.

Jayne didn't like taking breaks. They spoiled her fantasy. It was worse even than being at the agency during office hours, and that in itself was pretty hard on her feminine ego.

Nevertheless, Jayne, with Mr. Waterman's blessing, had spent the first part of this week at the agency with Garrett devising a strategy for rebuilding the company. It was a solid, conservative plan that depended on a little luck. And a lot of luck wouldn't be amiss, she thought carrying a stack of binders over to her coffee table.

Garrett had called the rest of the Charles family for a meeting. In Jayne's office. Today. They'd flown in from New York last night probably expecting a miracle. Jayne hoped to give them one.

"You mean there are more like him?" Sylvia peeled the paper cup away from her apple muffin and dug at a walnut.

"The whole family models."

"Wow."

Jayne scooped the ashtray out of Sylvia's reach. "Could you take your walnuts with you?"

Sylvia had been in the process of dropping the walnut and it now bounced on Jayne's coffee table. She gave Jayne a look.

"I'm going to have people in here, Sylvia. Models. I don't want pieces of walnuts in the ashtray."

"So I'll dump them in the trash."

"No!"

"Why not?"

"I don't want food smell in my office. Garrett's family is probably hungry all the time and it might distract them. I need them to concentrate."

"*Ooookay.*" Sylvia made a point of dropping the walnut pieces one by one into the white paper bag from the bakery.

Actually, Jayne was afraid of being distracted, herself. She'd given up her ten o'clock doughnut after being at Garrett's agency and her body was still adjusting—she hoped by shrinking. However, yesterday, she'd caught herself actually thinking about eating

Sylvia's walnut pieces out of the ashtray. She unwrapped a stick of gum and chewed hard.

Gum just wasn't the same as a chocolate doughnut.

Jayne fussed around her office, arranging and rearranging the Pace Waterman binders into which she'd put a complete financial analysis of the books, the disposition of the funds prior to George Windom's departure and the unfortunate disposition of funds *after* his departure. She had illustrated them with colorful graphs. She'd obsessed with borders and fonts, trying to make the unpalatable more palatable. All in all, she'd spent untold hours preparing for this meeting—untold, because she wasn't about to report the actual number to Mr. Waterman and have him bill Garrett after it was Jayne's idea to try to salvage Venus, Inc.

Her weekends and evenings were her own, or should be, anyway. If she wanted to devote them to Garrett, then she would. And she had.

"I thought the fan shape looked nice," Sylvia commented and brushed her hands together, scattering crumbs.

"Sylvia!" Jayne swiped at the chair cushions.

"Jayne…can I meet them?"

"This isn't a social occasion." Due to client confidentiality, Jayne hadn't told Sylvia anything about Garrett's situation. Sylvia was of the opinion that client confidentiality didn't extend to *her,* but Jayne wouldn't budge and Sylvia was still miffed.

"I figured that, but…couldn't I take a coffee order?"

Jayne studied Sylvia, remembering how she'd

acted when she'd previously met Garrett. "The receptionist will bring in a tray with a thermal pot."

"I could do that," Sylvia said brightly.

"I don't think so." Jayne rearranged the binders in a fan shape so she could avoid looking at Sylvia.

But she could feel Sylvia looking at her.

"I thought we were friends."

"We are." Now Jayne looked at her. "But they're new clients and you don't even work here."

Sylvia stood. "You're afraid that Garrett will pay attention to me, aren't you?"

No, I'm afraid you'll pay attention to Garrett. "Some other time."

"Right, like there'll be another time." Bracelets jangling, Sylvia flounced out of Jayne's office.

Jayne felt guilty until she noticed the white paper bag with the walnuts in it that Sylvia had left behind. She grabbed it and was trying to find a trash can outside her office when she heard voices coming from Mr. Waterman's end of the hall. That had to be Garrett and his family.

Still carrying the bakery bag, Jayne scurried back into her office, stuffed it into her own trash and stood by the desk. No, that looked too awkward. She sat on the couch next to the binders.

Now she looked as if she didn't have anything to do. She should look busy and important and valued to inspire confidence in Garrett's family. She sat behind her desk, which was in an abnormally pristine state. No files, no papers. She needed props. Reaching into her drawer, Jayne withdrew the first thing her hand touched just as Mr. Waterman appeared in her doorway.

"Jayne?"

"Just finishing up this…" She looked down and was horrified to find she was holding the cruise brochure. Yanking open her pencil drawer, she tried to stuff the brochure out of sight, but it didn't fit in the narrow drawer. She ended up letting it slither to the floor as she stood and prepared to meet Garrett's family.

Garrett herded his family into Jayne's office. He'd suggested coming to her office rather than meeting at the agency because he'd wanted them to understand the gravity of their situation. Too, he thought Jayne would be more comfortable on her own turf.

Garrett caught her eye and gave her a quick smile as his family drifted around him. After working with her the past several days, his confidence in her abilities was unshakable. He didn't know how she'd done it, but she made him feel as if their strategy was as much his as it was hers. He guessed that "make the client have an emotional stake in the solution" was a device she'd learned in business psychology, but he didn't care. It worked.

During their long hours together, Garrett had caught himself wondering about Jayne, the woman, as much as Jayne, the accountant. She never mentioned a boyfriend, either past or present, so he assumed she was currently not dating. It would be difficult to have much of a social life with the kind of hours she worked.

He looked forward to their sessions because afterward, he felt revitalized. He'd considered seeing her after hours, except they'd been working so hard, there weren't any after hours. Maybe now that the bulk of the planning had been done, he'd take her to dinner. She certainly deserved a night out on the town.

Garrett was ready to get the meeting under way. His parents were chatting with Mr. Waterman about some place in France and the twins were sulking because they'd rather be hanging out in the designer boutiques in Pavilion. Both wore the pout they'd perfected. Since this was their trademark look, Garrett hoped Jayne couldn't tell that this pout was the genuine thing.

They slouched over to the couch and draped themselves against it, Sasha on the arm and Sandor next to her. It was their party pose.

Jayne remained behind her desk, mutely staring at them. Garrett wasn't surprised. Although they could look quite different if they chose, particularly when Sasha pulled her hair back and wore dramatic makeup, today they were emphasizing their "twinness." Dressed alike in white tunics and pants, and both with the same chin-length hair, they made a striking picture.

His entire family made a striking picture, which was fortunate given their current financial state.

Garrett had never been quite as striking. His features weren't as angular, he wasn't as tall and he didn't get the high-fashion jobs the way they did. He was more the Father's Day, sportsmen's catalog type, which was fine with him. But if he'd been seriously pursuing a modeling career, he'd have been frustrated. Whenever he was with his parents and the twins, people overlooked him, which didn't bother him, except today, with Jayne here.

He didn't want Jayne to meet Sandor. He didn't want to see her caught by the legendary appeal of his younger brother, but judging from the wide-eyed blank look on her face, Sandor had eclipsed him once again. He only hoped Jayne didn't drop something or hurt herself when she met him.

"Garrett, I'll let you introduce everyone to Jayne," Mr. Waterman said, and left them alone as Garrett had asked.

Everyone looked at the woman still standing behind the desk. Garrett's heart sank. It was worse than he'd thought. She couldn't even move.

Fine. He'd bring everyone to her. Gesturing for his brother and sister to join him, he approached her. "Jayne, these are my parents, James and Rebecca Charles."

Jayne managed a smile and shook their hands. So far, nothing had been knocked over. But she still had to meet Sandor.

"My sister, Sasha..."

Sasha nodded at her.

"...and my brother, Sandor."

Sandor gave her one of his heavy-lidded looks. When Jayne held out her hand, he took it in both of his.

Very few women could resist Sandor when he set out to captivate them, either from the printed page, or in person. There was nothing Garrett could do, except edge closer to the filing basket and pencil holder on Jayne's desk, ready to catch them when she knocked them over. He glanced behind her to make sure her chair was in place in case her knees gave out.

But Jayne gave Sandor a perfunctory smile and, if

Garrett wasn't mistaken, pulled her hand away. A smile tugged at the corner of his mouth.

"Thank you all for coming," she said, and gestured to the sofa without hitting anything or anyone. "If you'll take a seat around the coffee table, I've put binders there for each of you."

Jayne immune to Sandor? As his family pivoted toward the coffee table, Garrett watched her, but she wasn't looking at Sandor and she didn't knock anything over, not even when she reached for a pen and the folder from her desk. Then she met his eyes.

Inordinately pleased, he widened his smile.

And Jayne dropped her pen.

She was numb. She wasn't even sure she could hold on to her pen.

So these intimidatingly sophisticated, polished, elegant, glamorous people were Garrett's family. They were tall. Garrett was tall, but these people were *tall* tall.

They were also thin and had cheekbones so high, the makeup artist probably used a ladder. The clothes they wore looked deceptively simple—no doubt designer originals.

In her navy-blue suit, Jayne felt frumpy, lumpy and short. She wondered if she could make her presentation from behind her desk so they wouldn't see her hips.

No, of course, not. She snuck a glance at Garrett, to find him watching her intently.

"I told them that George had stolen the agency assets and that the police haven't got any leads," he said.

"How are they taking it?"

He looked over toward the sofa. "It hasn't affected them yet."

"I suppose it's going to take a while to sink in."

"No, I mean it hasn't made any difference in the way they live, so they're not concerned." He looked back at her. "They've still got the apartment in New York and the house here in Houston. They can buy what they want—"

"Not for long!"

Garrett drew a breath. "Convincing them of that will be your biggest challenge." He smiled encouragingly and touched her lightly on the shoulder. "But I know you can do it."

In the face of such confidence, Jayne nearly melted.

Okay. It was time. Holding the folder in front of her hips, Jayne approached the group sitting around her coffee table as Garrett pulled her desk chair over for her.

Yes, sitting would be best. She smiled her thanks and Garrett went over and took his place next to his father's chair.

Jayne's gaze swept the group. No one had made a move to look at the binders. That surprised her. Weren't they curious about their financial state?

Garrett was right. His family was in deep denial. Understandable, but it meant that she'd still have to get past all the protests and the are-you-sure-you-haven't-made-a-mistake comments.

She'd never liked the awkwardness of people coming to terms with financial shocks.

Maybe she should stand after all, hips or no hips. "If everyone will take a binder, we'll get started."

The twins each took a binder, opened it, flipped through a few pages, checked each other's, shrugged, then closed the binders and put them back on the table.

Jayne was fascinated. It looked like they'd choreographed their movements.

Garrett's father had his binder open on his lap and had propped a finger against his cheek, looking as if he was posing as a silver-haired executive.

Rebecca Charles smoothed the silky legs of her pantsuit before carefully setting the binder on her nearly nonexistent thighs. She didn't open it.

Fine. Jayne would spoon-feed information to them. "Garrett came to me when he noticed irregularities in the Venus accounts after your business manager resigned."

"That was clever of you, Garrett," his mother said, smiling without crinkling her eyes. "I've always said that you were the clever one."

"Yes, that's what you've said." There was a faint impatience in Garrett's voice.

Here came the tricky part. "In addition, Mr. Windom withdrew almost all your liquid assets, including those held in escrow. I conducted an audit of the books and found that, in my opinion, the financial statements do not fairly represent the company's actual financial situation." Jayne waited for them to absorb the information. She'd used the technical legal language that basically called George Windom a liar.

Four pairs of pale blue eyes blinked at her, then looked at Garrett.

He straightened. "She's telling you that George stole all our money. Checking, savings, he cleaned out the agency, then tried to cover it up. When he couldn't, he left.''

"You told us that already," James Charles said.

"And you said that the police were looking for him." Rebecca Charles sounded as though she thought the money would be recovered at any moment.

"They are, but Jayne is just making sure you understand that, of this moment, the accounts are empty.''

"That's why I had to transfer money to you," Sasha said with a let's-get-on-with-it gesture. "So what are we doing here?''

"Yeah, you said it was a loan," Sandor added.

"Exactly," Jayne said. "Copies of the affidavit stating that you and Sasha lent money to Venus are in the binder, and I've worked out a repayment schedule. The loan met the agency's immediate obligations. In the meantime, Garrett and I have worked out a business plan to keep your company going until the funds are recovered. And I must stress that there is the possibility that they won't be.''

"No kiddin'. If I'd stolen a wad of cash like that, I sure wouldn't sit on it. It would be *par-tay* all day!'' Sandor wagged his index fingers from side to side.

Sasha laughed her agreement.

Mr. Charles closed the binder and returned it to the coffee table. "Whatever you and Garrett have decided is fine with us.''

"Go to it, bro!" Sasha jumped up and tugged at Sandor's arm. "Let's go have a sea salt scrub at Urban Retreat.''

"Wait!" Jayne protested with a helpless look at Garrett. "I haven't started yet."

"Sash, Sandy, go sit down." Garrett intercepted his brother and sister and turned them back to the sofa.

Jayne realized she was going to have to be very blunt and very basic. These people didn't have a clue.

"On pages eight through thirteen, you'll find a monthly breakdown of the agency's operating expenses during the last quarter with the income on the facing page. Included in the totals is income from the assets Mr. Windom has withdrawn. They are printed in red ink. On pages fourteen and fifteen, you'll find a revised monthly statement without the income from those assets. Should your expenses keep increasing at the average rate they have been over the past—"

Jayne was interrupted by a knock. Judging by the glassy expressions on the Charleses' faces, this wasn't a bad thing.

"Coffee anyone?"

Sylvia. She started to come into the office, but Jayne's glare kept her near the doorway. This was stretching the bonds of friendship way too far.

"I'd like a decaf skim milk cappuccino with cinnamon," Sasha piped up.

"Ditto." Sandor shifted his position and crossed his arms.

Everyone else nodded, so Jayne said, "Decaf skim milk cappuccinos for six." She smiled. Sylvia would have to hike through the walkway to the coffee shop in the mall to get the fancy coffees. Even if she bought the small sizes, it would still do serious damage to a twenty-dollar bill.

Served her right.

With a chagrined, but unrepentant expression, Sylvia backed out of Jayne's office and Jayne prepared to continue her presentation.

Garrett spoke first. "To summarize, Jayne is saying that our income has dropped and we need to make more money."

"Yes, but it's more compli—" Belatedly Garrett's look registered. *Simplify,* it said.

After that, they fell into a pattern of Jayne barely touching on the pages in the binders and Garrett translating into elementary language until at last, James Charles held up a hand.

"All this tells me is that we need to make more money."

"Yes," Garrett said.

"And cut expenses," Jayne reminded them, but no one paid any attention because a flushed Sylvia chose that moment to kick the door open.

"I hope that's the coffee," Sasha said.

"Twenty-two dollars and seventy-three cents," Sylvia murmured as she walked past Jayne with the cardboard tray.

"You sprang for the large size?"

"Wouldn't want them to think you were stingy," Sylvia said, glaring at Jayne before beaming a huge smile at Garrett.

"Hello again," she said in an overly bright voice that made Jayne cringe. "Coffee?"

"Thanks." Garrett took two paper cups and handed them to his parents.

Sylvia, standing as close as she could with the tray,

hungrily watched his every move. "What about you?"

"Go ahead and give my sister and brother theirs." He followed her over to the couch.

With each step he took, Jayne's spirits sank. Why couldn't she flirt like Sylvia? Why couldn't she attract men like Sylvia? Why couldn't she—

Sylvia stopped abruptly in front of the couch, a stunned look on her face as she encountered the twins.

"Hey, thanks." Sandor stood and reached across the table for the cups. After handing his sister one, he sat down and pried off the plastic lid, then sipped at the thin layer of foam, his pale blue eyes watching the immobile Sylvia. The tip of his tongue touched the edge of his mouth and Sylvia visibly swallowed.

Jayne saw the corner of the tray tilt a fraction of an inch and Garrett held out his hands, deftly rescuing the tray before Sylvia sank onto the coffee table, her gaze never leaving Sandor.

Garrett calmly carried the tray over to Jayne and offered her a coffee, taking the last one for himself.

Her friend had crashed an important client presentation and now sat smack-dab in the middle of the table, right on top of Mr. Charles's binder, if Jayne wasn't mistaken. She glanced around to see how everyone was taking this.

No one seemed to think anything was odd at having Sylvia stare at Sandor. Garrett's parents exchanged a few murmurs. Sasha drank her coffee and made a call on her cell phone.

"I apologize for Sylvia's intrusion," Jayne said, wondering how she was going to get her to leave without an embarrassing scene. Make that a *more* embarrassing scene.

"Not a problem. Sandor affects women that way."

"What? Turns them into drooling zombies?"

Garrett laughed softly. "Basically."

Jayne studied Garrett's younger brother as she sipped her coffee. Full lips pouted beneath a well-shaped nose. His cheekbones were so high they almost looked like a caricature. His eyebrows were thick and dark and his eyes a paler shade of Garrett's blue. Jayne had seen pictures of the twins at the agency, and frankly, thought they looked better in photographs than they did in person. They certainly weren't as good-looking as Garrett.

"I don't get it," she said at last, looking at Garrett.

He wore an unreadable expression as he searched her face. When he didn't say anything, Jayne thought she'd offended him.

Of *course* she'd offended him. Sandor was his brother and she'd just insulted—

"Jayne, if you haven't made other plans, will you have dinner with me tonight?"

Since the meeting had obviously deteriorated, reconvening for dinner was probably a good plan.

She headed for her desk. "I'm free, but let me check with Mr. Waterman. I know he'd like to be there."

As she set her cup down and reached for the telephone, Garrett stepped forward and covered her hand with his. "I don't want to have dinner with Jayne, the accountant," he said near her ear. "I want to have dinner with Jayne, the woman."

CHAPTER SIX

JAYNE, the woman, was flabbergasted. "You do?"

Garrett laughed softly. "Is that so hard to believe?"

"Well…yes."

"Why? We've spent days working long hours together and I'd like to get to know you better." His
voice was low so the others wouldn't hear.

He made having dinner with her sound so logical.
Jayne excelled at logic.

"I was thinking of making reservations at Nicky
V's for eight," he continued.

Nicky V's was a ritzy restaurant not too far from
her office. Jayne had never been there and had always
wanted to go, but it was a definite "date" restaurant.
Unfortunately, her dates didn't seem to know that.

"Eight will be fine. My car's in the Park & Ride,
so I'll have to meet you there," she whispered before
panicking.

She'd just agreed to go out with Garrett! Alone.
The two of them. Tonight.

She wanted to jump up and down and attract
Sylvia's attention so she could tell her all about it.

Except jumping up and down in front of Garrett
would be extremely uncool and besides Sylvia was
now on the sofa with Sandor and only a nuclear ex-
plosion would divert her attention.

Jayne would have to keep the knowledge all to herself for now. Her knees had gone all quivery. She ought to call the meeting back to order while she could still stand. She made a move toward the group.

"Just a minute." Garrett stepped in front of her. "You have a little milk foam right—" he took his finger and gently touched the corner of her upper lip "—there."

Jayne's heart was beating so hard, she thought Garrett must surely hear it. Her lip tingled and she was starting to see dark spots.

But they went away as soon as she realized she wasn't breathing and took a deep breath.

Garrett was still standing close to her and looking at her in a way that would fuel her dreams for weeks.

She might never have moved, except Jayne, the accountant, had taken over and had wrapped up the meeting with Garrett's family. They truly weren't interested in knowing the operating details of their company, and had eagerly signed over voting proxies to Garrett, which meant he and Jayne could begin putting their plan into place at once.

And Sylvia? Sylvia had walked out clinging to Sandor, which meant that Jayne couldn't consult with her over what to wear or how to do her hair or anything.

Actually Jayne didn't have much of a choice of what to wear. The only time she really dressed up was when she attended the annual Pace Waterman Christmas dinner. For this, she had a black wool suit. In deference to the festive occasion, there was black beading on the lapels and with it, Jayne wore a red silk charmeuse blouse.

But this was June and it was ninety degrees outside.

An Important Message from the Editors

Dear Reader,

Because you've chosen to read one of our fine romance novels, we'd like to say "thank you!" And, as a <u>special</u> way to thank you, we've selected <u>two more</u> of the books you love so well, <u>plus</u> an exciting mystery gift, to send you absolutely FREE!

Please enjoy them with our compliments...

Candy Lee

Editor

P.S. And because we <u>value</u> our customers, we've attached something extra inside...

Peel off seal and Place inside...

How to validate your
Editor's FREE GIFT "Thank You"

1. Peel off gift seal from front cover. Place it in space provided at right. This automatically entitles you to receive two free books and a fabulous mystery gift.

2. Send back this card and you'll get brand-new Harlequin Romance® novels. These books have a cover price of $3.50 each in the U.S. and $3.99 each in Canada, but they are yours to keep absolutely free.

3. There's no catch. You're under no obligation to buy anything. We charge nothing—ZERO—for your first shipment. And you don't have to make any minimum number of purchases—not even one!

4. The fact is thousands of readers enjoy receiving books by mail from the Harlequin Reader Service®. They like the convenience of home delivery...they like getting the best new novels BEFORE they're available in stores... and they love our discount prices!

5. We hope that after receiving your free books you'll want to remain a subscriber. But the choice is yours— to continue or cancel, any time at all! So why not take us up on our invitation, with no risk of any kind. You'll be glad you did!

6. Don't forget to detach your FREE BOOKMARK. And remember...just for validating your Editor's Free Gift Offer, we'll send you THREE gifts, *ABSOLUTELY FREE!*

GET A FREE MYSTERY GIFT...

YOURS FREE!

SURPRISE MYSTERY GIFT COULD BE YOURS _FREE_ AS A SPECIAL "THANK YOU" FROM THE EDITORS OF HARLEQUIN

The Editor's "Thank You" Free Gifts Include:

- ● Two BRAND-NEW romance novels!
- ● An exciting mystery gift!

PLACE FREE GIFT SEAL HERE

YES! I have placed my Editor's "Thank You" seal in the space provided above. Please send me 2 free books and a fabulous mystery gift. I understand I am under no obligation to purchase any books, as explained on the back and on the opposite page.

316 HDL CQTU

116 HDL CQTE
(H-R-06/99)

Name: _____
PLEASE PRINT

Address: _____ Apt.#: _____

City: _____

State/Prov.: _____ Postal Zip/Code: _____

Thank You!

The Harlequin Reader Service® — Here's how it works:

Accepting your 2 free books and mystery gift places you under no obligation to buy anything. You may keep the books and gift and return the shipping statement marked "cancel." If you do not cancel, about a month later we'll send you 6 additional novels and bill you just $2.90 each in the U.S., or $3.34 each in Canada, plus 25¢ delivery per book and applicable taxes if any.* That's the complete price and — compared to the cover price of $3.50 in the U.S. and $3.99 in Canada — it's quite a bargain! You may cancel at any time, but if you choose to continue, every month we'll send you 6 more books, which you may either purchase at the discount price or return to us and cancel your subscription.

*Terms and prices subject to change without notice. Sales tax applicable in N.Y. Canadian residents will be charged applicable provincial taxes and GST.

And this was Garrett, not Mr. Waterman and the Pace Waterman accounting staff.

She wanted something pretty, not something business dressy. She needed Sylvia to come shopping with her, but Sylvia had apparently disappeared. She wasn't at her desk when Jayne called her to see if she wanted to go to lunch. Maybe it was just as well, since Jayne still had to have it out with her over barging in on the meeting.

Jayne decided to go shopping by herself and was promptly overwhelmed by the choices. Everything was so…bare and sheer. So un-Jayne-like.

Finally, in the relative anonymity of a large department store, she fled to the dressing room with a suit in familiar and comfortable black—not in wool—which had quilted satin lapels. As soon as she had it on, she felt better, more in control. Calmer.

In spite of what Garrett said, in spite of the way he'd looked at her, Jayne knew this was a business dinner. It couldn't be anything else.

Turning, she looked at the back of the skirt in the mirror. It was shorter than she was used to wearing and the slit was at least eight inches long, instead of a more conservative two- or three-inch slit.

The jacket was meant to be worn without a blouse. Jayne stared at the white V of her throat and pulled the lapels closer together. As soon as she let go, the lapels settled back into their original position.

On the plus side, when she spread her arms and wiggled her shoulders, the lapels didn't pull apart very far.

For anyone else, the suit would be conservative.

For Jayne, revealing her throat was daring, not to mention the slit in the back of the skirt.

She bought the outfit, feeling quite pleased with herself.

As soon as she got back to her office, she called Sylvia, who *still* wasn't there. After that Jayne didn't call anymore since she didn't want to draw attention to Sylvia's continued absence with a ringing phone. Yes, she was angry with Sylvia, but she didn't want to get her fired.

Jayne spent the rest of the afternoon concentrating on the business plan for Garrett's company. This way, she knew she'd have something to talk about should the dinner conversation lag. She still wasn't entirely ready to accept that this was a social occasion and not a business one.

With the upcoming dinner foremost in her mind, Jayne had thought she wouldn't be able to concentrate this afternoon, but the hours evaporated. It was obvious to her that Garrett would need to hire a business manager at some point. Right now, he was acting as both booking agent and business manager, but one of their plans was to increase the list of models they represented. Jayne could handle the business part, but her own regular client list, which Mr. Waterman had temporarily assigned to Bill Pellman, was extensive. She didn't have an extra four hours a day to spend on Garrett's business. Besides, at the hourly rates Pace Waterman charged for their services, it wasn't going to be financially feasible for long.

Jayne made a note to suggest that he hire a part-time accountant, such as a mother who wanted to work from her home while her children were small.

Jayne knew several of her former colleagues who wanted to keep up with the industry, but weren't willing to put in the long hours being an associate of an accounting firm required. In the past, she'd had success matching several of them with smaller businesses. Everybody won in those instances.

Speaking of long hours... Jayne looked at her watch. Today, she planned to leave at the nominal quitting hour of five-thirty. Since her car was in the Park & Ride lot, she planned to take the bus out west to retrieve it and meet Garrett at the restaurant.

She was packing up her files when the intercom on her phone buzzed.

"Jayne?" It was Mr. Waterman's secretary. "He'd like to see you in his office if it's convenient."

Which meant now, unless she was meeting with a client. "Be there in a few minutes," she said, hoping this wasn't going to take long. She wanted plenty of time to prepare for dinner with Garrett. If she gave it some attention, her hair was actually not too bad these days.

Mr. Waterman wasn't alone. An extremely smug Bill Pellman sat in one of the plush leather chairs next to the desk.

"Jayne, I'm aware that you've taken an interest in young Bill's career, so I wanted you to be the first to know that I've promoted him to executive accountant."

"Executive accountant?" Jayne repeated dumbly. Bill had only been with Pace Waterman a year and a half.

It had taken Jayne five years to reach that level. In fact, she'd only been *senior* executive accountant for just the past six months, and that was after putting in thousands of hours of overtime.

"Yes." Mr. Waterman had an unlit celebratory cigar in his mouth.

So did Bill.

Jayne wasn't offered a cigar. She wouldn't have accepted one, but it would have been nice to have been asked.

"Bill has handled your client list quite admirably lately."

"I'm glad the past *week* hasn't been too difficult for him," Jayne said, making sure she emphasized "week." Anybody could handle anything for a week.

"And I'm especially pleased with his work on the Magruder report. He found an error that had been perpetuated for three months."

Which was how long Bill had been responsible for the Magruder report. Jayne suspected the error had been his in the first place. She leveled a look at him. "I'm glad my memo on the subject was of help to you."

Bill only grinned around his cigar.

"Yes, that and the six new accounts he brought in after teaching only one course of the accounting seminars, and I knew we were looking at executive accountant material."

Six? *Six?* Jayne had brought in *dozens* over the years. Besides, hadn't those accounts come after *her* lectures this last session? And *she'd* found the Magruder mistake.

Mr. Waterman stood to shake Bill's hand. "I see a senior executive in the not-too-distant future."

"Would that be to fill a vacancy caused by some-

one's promotion to vice president?'' Jayne asked
more to put the idea into Mr. Waterman's head than
because she thought that was the case.

He chuckled. ''Vice president has a nice ring to it.
Right, Bill?''

Bill mimicked Waterman's chuckle. ''Sure, but,
Jayne, I'm not quite ready for a vice presidency.''

''Oh, I know,'' Jayne said, biting off her words.
''But there are others of us who are.''

Mr. Waterman all but patted her on the head. ''If
they work as hard as Bill has, then we'll see.''

Like *that* would be a challenge. Jayne wanted to
snatch that cigar out of Mr. Waterman's mouth and
stomp on it.

Unfortunately she understood. She'd always understood, but until now, she'd believed she could over-
come Mr. Waterman's prejudice with outstanding
work.

But she was a woman. Bill was a man—and a wea-
selly one at that. She had a feeling that he'd be promoted to senior executive before she made vice president. If ever.

It was time to remind Mr. Waterman of all she'd
done for the company lately. ''Congratulations, Bill.
I know you're pleased.'' Turning to Mr. Waterman,
she said, ''The meeting with the Charles family went
well today. They gave preliminary approval to our
business plan. I'll write up a status report for you after
I meet with Garrett Charles this evening.''

''Perhaps Bill should sit in on the meeting,'' Mr.
Waterman suggested.

Jayne froze. *No!* Bill was *not* going to horn in on
ner dinner with Garrett! Her mind raced. ''Since he's

covering my other clients, Bill's workload is much too heavy to take on the Venus account.''

"But I should familiarize myself with the account.'' Bill leaned back in the chair and watched her as he toyed with his cigar. He'd figured out that she didn't want him along.

"You're absolutely correct," Jayne said, surprising him. "You should familiarize yourself with *all* the accounts in our department.''

His fingers stilled.

"It will have to be off-hours, you know, evenings and weekends, since Mr. Waterman can't, in good conscience, bill the clients for your time.''

Bill's eyes darted to Mr. Waterman who was nodding in agreement.

Jayne smiled. "I think we can give Bill a break tonight, can't we, Mr. Waterman?''

Mr. Waterman waved his cigar magnanimously.

"Thanks," a subdued Bill managed to say.

"Come see me in the morning," Jayne said and left the office feeling that she'd gotten a little of her own back.

She had only herself to blame for creating Bill, the accounting wonder boy. She could hardly fault him for taking advantage of her help and accepting the offered promotion.

He was going to be a problem, but she would deal with that tomorrow. Right now, she had to hurry, or she would be late for her dinner with Garrett.

Garrett saw Jayne before she saw him. He'd been sitting on a stool at the edge of the bar where he could see the doorway and he watched her hurry toward the outer glass doors from the parking lot. Her curls bounced and gleamed in the sunlight and she wore a black suit that immediately reminded him of a curvy forties movie star. He unconsciously reached up to straighten his tie, but he'd gone the collarless shirt route tonight.

He was looking forward to the evening even more than he looked forward to the days she worked at the agency. He'd always known that he wanted to concentrate on the business aspect of his family's agency, but George Windom had sapped his confidence and made him doubt his abilities.

Jayne had restored his self-assurance and more. After working with her the past week, he knew he had the capability to run the agency. All he lacked was experience dealing with the financial aspects, but Jayne's business plan compensated for it.

She was brilliant, capable, numerically self-assured…and was possibly the one woman in the entire world who was immune to Sandor.

Garrett liked that in a woman.

It must have been a trick of the setting sun, but Jayne saw Garrett's eyes light up when he spotted her. She glanced behind her to see if he'd seen someone else, but only found the parking attendant. When she looked back, he'd walked down the pink marble steps to meet her and she decided that his blue eyes held a polite pleasure, nothing more. Just because he'd invited her to dinner didn't mean he was romantically interested in her.

"You look great," he said and greeted her with a continental kiss.

During Jayne's days at the agency, she'd seen a lot of such kissing going on and knew not too make too much of it, but here she was in a new outfit that made her feel elegant, being kissed by the most gorgeous man in the universe for all to see.

Pretty fantastic, now that she thought about it.

The gentle pressure of Garrett's hand in the small of her back as they followed the hostess to their table gave Jayne a warm feeling in the pit of her stomach. Would it be so terrible to pretend—just a little—as long as Garrett didn't suspect?

Mirrors tiled the back wall of the restaurant. Jayne could see the handsome man behind her, and the way women's eyes swiveled and watched their progress across the room. Garrett would always draw women's eyes, she thought.

"Garrett!" cried a female voice. And then, incredibly, "Oh, and Jayne! Hi!"

Jayne searched for the speaker and saw Micky, the receptionist from Venus, sitting two tables away with three other young, overly attractive people—the sort who normally intimidated Jayne.

But Micky wore a wide, all inclusive smile as she introduced Garrett to them as her boss, and Jayne as the Venus accountant who "knows everything there is to know about numbers. When I start making real money, she's the one *I'm* going to hire," Micky told the others.

"That will be the best decision you'll ever make," Garrett said, smiling down at Jayne.

Pleased, she felt herself blushing.

Micky chattered on for a bit, then made shooing motions with her hands. "Anyway, you two go on to your table. You deserve a night out after all the time you've spent cooped up in the office."

Garrett raised a hand in farewell and immediately steered Jayne toward the waiting hostess.

"Micky seems nice," Jayne said as she slid onto the gold velvet banquette against the wall. The fabric caught the material of her skirt and raised it a few inches above her knees. "She's gone out of her way to be helpful while I've been at the agency."

"She's a sweet kid," he agreed, taking the chair opposite her.

Jayne surreptitiously tugged at her skirt hem. There was no way to pull it back to where she wanted it without drawing attention to what she was doing. But who was going to see? The tablecloth covered her legs. She left her wayward skirt alone. "Doesn't Micky want to model? She looks like she could."

"We book her locally when we can, but her boyfriend doesn't like her traveling or working weekends. She was all set to head for Europe this summer and build her portfolio until she hooked up with him."

Nicky V's had capitalized on its current popularity by adding extra tables and it was packed tonight and noisy tonight. Jayne leaned closer so she wouldn't feel as if she was shouting. "Is her boyfriend one of the men we met?"

Garrett's gaze dipped downward before he shook his head. "No. I saw him once when he came to pick her up after work. He's more the football player type." His eyes flickered downward again.

All at once, Jayne remembered her neckline and the fact that she wasn't wearing a blouse. Sitting up abruptly, she grabbed the menu to hide the fact that he'd flustered her.

"Yes, I suppose we'd better decide what we're going to order," he said mildly.

When Jayne peeked at him over the menu, she swore she saw him smiling.

What if he thought she'd leaned over on purpose? What if he thought she was flirting with him? How embarrassing. No more pretending. Men like Garrett did not, except in fairy tales, end up with Plain Janes. So, until she got home, she was going to be all business.

"See anything you like?" Garrett asked and Jayne realized she'd been staring at the menu without reading anything on it.

"I, ah…" Good grief. Every entrée had an explanatory paragraph beneath it. Words like "goat cheese," "endive," "jicama" and lots of purees of this and essences of that jumped at her. What if she mispronounced one of them? Where was "fried" or "baked" or plain old "sauce"? She knew how to pronounce those.

Obviously she was way out of the restaurant loop. She should pay more attention when Sylvia went on about her dates.

"Do you like fish?" Garrett asked.

"Fish is…okay," she said, trying to figure out if *he* liked fish.

"The sea bass is good here."

"Then I'll give that a try." Honestly, if Garrett had suggested pan-seared shoe leather with puree of mango spiked with cilantro, she would have agreed.

With the ordering hurdle out of the way, Jayne decided to bring up the topic of Venus's new business plan. Folding her hands on the table to remind herself not to lean forward, she began with a polite, "I enjoyed meeting your family today."

He grinned. "You look so serious. Don't be. I know you're thinking that they didn't pay much attention to what we said, but realistically, you can't expect them to instantly absorb financial data that took us a week to generate."

She hoped they'd absorbed the fact that they were broke.

"They have different strengths, which you'll see when we interview new talent. And my parents have so many contacts they can place almost anyone."

Jayne felt ashamed of herself because she *had* thought the Charleses, with the exception of Garrett, were mental lightweights. Garrett was right. She wouldn't know the first thing about acquiring models and if they sat her down and started spouting information at her, she'd probably be bored, too. "I just want them to fully understand what we're doing because..." She trailed off. *That* was a road she shouldn't be going down, either.

Garrett leaned forward. "Because of George."

Jayne nodded, remaining stiffly upright.

"Sasha actually figured out what happened there." Before she realized what he was doing, he stood, moved between their table and the one next to it, and joined her on the velvet banquette. "This is better," he said settling into place. "We could hardly hear each other."

Two people weren't meant to sit on this side of the table, but that apparently didn't bother Garrett. His leg was pressed up against hers and her skirt was halfway up her thigh. He drew his arm across the back of the banquette behind her. "As I said, Sasha's figured out what happened with George."

Jayne could feel the heat of Garrett's body and the hard length of his leg. Her leg was hard, too, but that was due to the black, industrial-strength-support-and-control-top panty hose she was wearing and not muscle. She hoped he couldn't tell the difference.

"It sounds like his problem was a plain, garden variety inferiority complex," Garrett said. "Sasha said he was hitting on the models—he even asked her out and he must be thirty or thirty-five years older than she is. She says he wasn't having much luck and I gather it became somewhat of a joke around the office."

"And you think he knew?"

Garrett reached across the table for his wineglass. "I not only think he knew, I think he became jealous and resentful and tried to compensate by making risky investments in hopes they'd pay off big and he'd have a lot of money to flash around."

"Except it wasn't his money."

"It was at first, but he ran into trouble, borrowed from Venus and never could pay it back."

That made sense. Jayne hadn't been able to figure out what would motivate a business manager into making such speculative investments. There wasn't any need and the risk was too high. "He knew you'd eventually discover what he'd been doing, so he left."

"Right. While you were working out the figures last week, I compared dates and timing. He was running our billing receipts through another account before depositing them in escrow. He'd dip into the market for a few hours, sell and then deposit the original amount into our escrow fund."

More laws George had broken. "And everything was great as long as he made money."

"Right." Garrett took a sip of his wine. "Do you realize that we've spent the evening so far talking about me and my family and the business when I really wanted to learn about you?" As he spoke, he slipped his arm off the banquette onto her shoulder.

And here Jayne thought she'd been dealing admirably with having Garrett sitting as close as possible. He'd seemed laid-back and matter-of-fact about it, so she'd tried to be casual as well. She'd made conversation and everything. True, she hadn't attempted to drink her wine, or even water because every time she moved, her skirt slid farther up her leg, but she didn't think he'd noticed.

She could only imagine how she looked, with her hands clasped tightly in her lap, providing an anchor for the skirt, while Garrett sprawled comfortably next to her.

"So tell me about you," Garrett prompted.

Jayne thought she could risk handling the wineglass. She reached forward, felt her skirt ease and started talking. "I've been with Pace Waterman for over six ye—" She'd leaned back and discovered herself against Garrett's shoulder. She shifted, but Garrett held her fast.

"This is more comfortable. You're fine here, aren't you?"

No, she was not fine! How could she be fine when every second she spent nestled against him, surrounded by his warmth became a struggle to keep from flinging her arms around him and saying, "Kiss me, you fool"?

Jayne took a swallow of her wine. "Six years. I've been with Pace Waterman for six years," she said determinedly.

"What do you do when you aren't an accountant with Pace Waterman?"

"I—" What did she do? Watch TV? Go out to eat or to the movies with Sylvia? Have the odd blind date here and there? "I think about being an accountant with Pace Waterman."

Garrett laughed, a low, intimate chuckle that Jayne felt as well as heard. "I'll have to give you something else to think about." His look made her shiver.

"Oh, you have!" Jayne blurted out without fully thinking her answer through.

"And what is that?"

You. She swallowed. "Well, Sylvia and I are planning a cruise."

Garrett thought for a moment. "Sylvia is your friend who's with Sandor."

"I guess that's where she is," Jayne grumbled.

"She is. They've gone clubbing."

There was a tone in Garrett's voice she couldn't identify. "Is there something wrong with that?"

Shaking his head, Garrett set his glass on the table. "I wouldn't worry about her. My impression is that your friend has had experience with the type of man Sandor is."

"What type is that?"

"The fun-for-the-moment type. Now if he were with you, I'd worry."

Jayne made a face. "Because I'm not a fun-for-the-moment type?"

"Because you'd get hurt. Sandor's interest never lasts long."

"And you think that won't hurt Sylvia?"

"Sylvia looks like she knows when to protect her emotions. You haven't learned how yet."

He was right, but Jayne didn't like him being right. It meant he was too perceptive for comfort. Meant he might know how he was affecting her. "Have you learned to protect *your* emotions?" she asked to divert the conversation away from her.

He nodded. "You learn quick in the modeling business."

Before Jayne could question him further, their waiter arrived with a stuffed mushroom appetizer Garrett had ordered to split with her. Instead of moving back to his seat the way Jayne expected him to, he signaled the waiter to move his place setting.

With his arm no longer around her shoulders, Jayne eased to one side a bit, which twisted her skirt. Why hadn't she realized before that velvet was such a vicious fabric?

As soon as the waiter had set her plate in front of her, Jayne saw why Garrett had wanted to split the dish. Half a grilled portabello mushroom with a generous lump of crabmeat sat on a green nest. Jayne liked mushrooms as well as anyone, but this was a lot of mushroom.

She picked up her fork and put a tiny bit of the crabmeat on it.

"No, no." Garrett took the fork from her. "You

need to experience all the flavors simultaneously. Let me.''

As Jayne watched, Garrett speared a little greenery, shaved off a bit of mushroom and managed to balance a flake or two of crabmeat on the fork. Then he held it out to her.

Jayne made as though to take it in her hand, but with an amused look he murmured, ''Open your mouth.''

Jayne did, more from surprise than anything else.

Slowly Garrett set the fork on her tongue and Jayne closed her mouth around it. Just as slowly, he withdrew the fork. ''How is it?''

She'd forgotten to register the taste. Quickly chewing, she swallowed. ''It's good.''

''Too fast.'' Garrett created another bite for her. ''This time, savor the taste.''

He held her gaze as she slowly chewed and swallowed. ''Well?''

Jayne smiled and nodded, glad speech wasn't required.

''There.'' He gave her back her fork.

Although Jayne took tiny stacked bites and swallowed them slowly, she didn't really appreciate the chef's combination of flavors.

She was thinking about Garrett. He was being...nice to her. Or something. She had to remember that in his world, people were more flamboyant in their actions. Hadn't he already warned her to protect her emotions?

Except Jayne was afraid that where Garrett was concerned, his warning had come too late.

CHAPTER SEVEN

GARRETT took in Jayne's stiff body posture and mentally shook his head. He'd done everything but draw her an equation to let her know he was interested in her.

Maybe he *should* draw her an equation.

He'd never met anyone as determinedly unresponsive. He didn't believe it was because she wasn't attracted to him. He couldn't be misreading the signals. No, when he remembered their first several meetings, the signals had been endearingly clear. The problem was now, she wasn't signaling back.

She didn't yet realize he was interested in *her.*

Was she still hung up on his looks? Garrett felt a fleeting disappointment. He'd been judged on his looks his entire life; it was a reality of the business he was in. By the same token, he'd learned to look beyond people's appearances to the person they were inside. He yearned to find someone who could do so as well. Someone who would like and love him for himself, not the way he looked. After working with Jayne for so many hours, he'd thought their comfortable working relationship could expand to a personal one.

But Jayne was obviously having difficulty with the transition.

"You were going to tell me about yourself," he prompted, not ready to give up yet.

She immediately dropped her fork and put on her serious expression. He supposed he shouldn't tell her that she looked cute when she did so, but she did.

"I graduated at the top of my class at—"

"Jayne," he interrupted her gently. "I'm already convinced that you're a stellar accountant. I want to know everything else about you."

She looked at a loss.

Garrett flung out a handful of conversational starters. "Do you travel? What kind of books do you like to read? Any hobbies or hidden talents? If you could go back in time and have dinner with anyone, who would it be and why?"

He expected her to laugh and pick one. Instead, gazing off into the distance, she recited her answers. "I went to Mexico with my parents once."

Garrett started to comment, but Jayne continued before he had a chance.

"I read financial journals, magazines and newspapers mostly, but I used to like science fiction. My only unusual talent is that if you tell me a date, I can tell you what day of the week it is and I'd like to go back in time and have dinner with my birth parents." When she finished, she looked back at him inquiringly. "Is that the sort of information you wanted?"

She'd distilled a potential thirty minutes of conversation into a few seconds. Nonplussed, Garrett stared at her. "Jayne, this isn't an interview."

"What do you mean?"

He gestured. "I want a little more conversational give and take. You mentioned 'birth' parents. Does that mean you're adopted?"

She nodded. "My parents were middle-aged when they adopted me."

Aha, a clue. "No brothers or sisters?"

She shook her head.

The only child of no doubt adoring older parents. Garrett began to understand where her serious demeanor came from, although she could have just as easily been spoiled. "Do you often think about finding your birth parents?"

"Oh, no!"

She looked upset and he could tell that she didn't want him to think she felt any disloyalty to the parents who'd raised her.

"They were teenagers and couldn't take care of a baby. I figure they've both made new lives. Of course, I wonder what they looked like. And it would be interesting to sit and talk with them, just to find out what kind of people they were then. But now—" she raised a shoulder "—they'd just be strangers."

After she revealed that glimpse into her background, Garrett had better luck in drawing her out. During their meal, he slowly and carefully chipped away at her reserve and gradually, Jayne relaxed around him, opening up more and more.

As they talked over coffee, he was even able to put his arm behind her again without her holding herself stiffly upright.

He enjoyed the feel of her against him, with her soft curves and creamy skin. He liked watching her talk, enjoyed the way her small, well-formed mouth moved.

He liked what she had to say, too, and the way she

listened to his views and opinions, feeling free to agree or disagree.

In fact, it was when she was disagreeing with him that he found her most attractive because it demonstrated that what he thought mattered to her. His appearance wasn't a factor in the discussion.

Too, with Jayne, he knew he wouldn't have to talk about any of the aspects of the fashion world, which made up the bulk of the conversations with his family and those who worked at the agency.

The restaurant was less than a quarter full when Jayne refused a third refill of coffee and looked at her watch. "It's almost eleven o'clock!"

Garrett was pleased to hear the surprise in her voice. That meant she'd enjoyed herself, too. "I suppose we'd better go," he agreed reluctantly. "But let's do this again. Soon."

When she nodded, he stepped away from the banquette and turned to help her.

Jayne hesitated, then pulled her napkin off her lap revealing a length of black-stockinged thigh. Garrett swallowed, mesmerized, as she put her hand in his.

As soon as she stood, her skirt fell back into place, but all Garrett could think about was the provocative glimpse of her leg.

There was something tantalizing about seeing Jayne's leg, a vaguely illicit sexiness. He was fascinated, and he didn't know why. It was only her leg and she'd reveal more of it in a pair of shorts, so that wasn't the reason. Maybe it was because she hadn't intended for him to see that part of her leg. He'd seen a lot of legs, but he hadn't seen *Jayne's* leg. He'd spent the better part of the evening with that leg pressed against his, oblivious to the fact that her skirt was no longer covering it.

Delayed reaction, that's what it was.

He followed her out of the restaurant, watching the sway of her hips. She wore high heels, which did lovely things to her walk. With each step, the slit in her skirt opened and he could see shadowy flashes a few inches above her knees.

Garrett had a thing for forties-era glamour and Jayne in her retro suit and high heels had pretty much hit his hot buttons.

He walked her to her car, aware that he hadn't said anything since they'd stepped into the moist night air. It was more enjoyable to walk behind her.

"This is it," she said unnecessarily, since there weren't any other cars surrounding the sensible dark gray sedan.

Still he said nothing, mutely watching as she beeped the alarm off and opened the door before he could.

She turned to face him. "I enjoyed dinner tonight. Thanks." She very properly held out her hand for him to shake.

Garrett took her hand, but he didn't shake it. He didn't want to shake it. He wanted to kiss her.

Jayne looked up at him questioningly, her lips slightly parted.

Gently, but insistently pulling her toward him, Garrett placed her hand on his shoulder, then curved his own around her waist and kissed her.

He expected surprise to hold her immobile and had anticipated her stiffening and pulling away.

He didn't expect Jayne's other arm to find its way

around his neck and for her to press her lips and her body against his.

Surprise held *him* immobile, but just for a fraction of a second. Then his arms tightened around her as he finally held her as close as he'd wanted to all evening.

For long moments, he simply enjoyed the feel of her in his arms. She wasn't long and bony like most of the women around the agency, and frankly, it was to her advantage. She looked lush and generous and warm and was revealing a sensual nature she'd kept hidden until now.

Her kiss was sweeter than he'd imagined, and he had an excellent imagination. Jayne's mouth was smaller and firmer than the puffy model lips popular right now. It was just right. He nibbled at her lower lip. More than right.

Her mouth was open against his and Garrett took full advantage. She tasted of the coffee they'd shared and something more that he knew was Jayne herself.

He deepened the kiss and she was right there with him, running her hands across his shoulders and threading them in the hair at the back of his neck.

They stayed there far too long, holding each other and kissing under the halogen parking lot lights until eventually Garrett's lust-soaked brain registered the delightful fact that Jayne was not going to be the one to break the kiss.

That meant he was going to have to break the kiss. He couldn't think of anything he wanted to do less, which was exactly the reason he should stop kissing her. Now. Or in just a little while...

He pulled back without his usual end-of-kiss finesse.

Jayne still had her eyes closed, lips parted and a dreamy expression on her face. Garrett desperately wanted to continue kissing her, but settled for dropping a light kiss on her forehead.

Her eyes blinked open. "Oh." Pulling her arms away awkwardly, she stepped back and bumped up against the car door, laughed self-consciously and ungracefully plopped onto the car seat.

The last thing Garrett saw was a flash of thigh as she swiveled her legs inside and shut the car door.

She'd imagined the whole thing.

That had to be the explanation.

Under the strain of the evening, of constantly striving to behave professionally, of reminding herself that she was at a business dinner and that Garrett wasn't responsible for, or aware of, her fantasies, and then sitting so close to him for so long, and he was so...so charming and nice to her and treating her to a lovely dinner as well as being incredibly handsome and... well... A lesser woman would have caved long before.

When she got to her car and it was time to say good-night, she was desperately wishing he'd kiss her good-night even though she knew she shouldn't and he wouldn't, and then she held out her hand and he'd looked down at her...

And then she'd kind of blanked out until he'd kissed her on the forehead. Like a ninny, she'd flung her arms around his neck and imagined the passionate kiss of her dreams, imagined his mouth on hers, his arms crushing her to his chest, his hand cupping the back of her head as his lips teased hers...

Well, maybe he'd think she'd just been steadying herself by lightly gripping his shoulders.

She hoped.

The next morning, Jayne stopped by Venus to pick up the books before going on to her office. She slipped in, waved at Micky and slipped back out. She wasn't trying to avoid Garrett, she told herself. She knew he was busy. It was the weekly open house at the agency and hopeful models already crowded the waiting room. Jayne would get more work done in the quiet of her own office.

It was well after nine-thirty when she passed by Bill's cubicle. She stopped when she saw it was empty and stripped of everything but a telephone and chair.

Then she remembered. Bill had been promoted. Terrific. She wondered where his new office was.

Her own office was empty. Although their usual meeting time was ten o'clock, she'd half expected Sylvia to be eagerly waiting to tell her about her evening. And maybe, night.

Her voice mail message light blinked. Nine messages. Concerned, Jayne dumped the files on her desk and didn't even put her purse away before picking up the receiver and listening to the messages.

The first three were from Bill asking a couple of questions, then wondering where she was. After that were calls from clients, a message from Mr. Waterman's secretary to call when she got in, another call from Bill, then Garrett chastising her for not saying hello when she'd been by this morning. She sighed, remembering last night. It was tempting to call him, but he'd be in the middle of interviewing models right now.

The last message was from Micky telling her that Bill had called the agency looking for her. None from Sylvia.

Jayne called Mr. Waterman back first. "Bill expressed concern when he was unable to locate you," he said.

Bill had tattled on her? Jayne gritted her teeth and explained where she'd been.

"Nevertheless, you should keep everyone informed when you'll be out of the office," Mr. Waterman said.

If the office couldn't manage without her for an hour, then she was more valuable to the company than she thought. She considered pointing this out to Mr. Waterman, but fortunately didn't.

Still, his words struck her the wrong way, so she wasn't in the best of moods when she called Bill.

"What's the problem?" she asked.

"Where have you been?" he snapped.

In spite of his promotion, she was still his supervisor. Jayne let the silence grow between them before replying, "Working." And she didn't elaborate.

"Listen, there's a problem with two of your accounts."

Jayne propped herself on the edge of her desk. "Two of the ones *you've* been handling?"

"Yeah, Modern Madrigals and The Village Smithy." Bill hesitated. "Okay, look. I missed a tax filing deadline."

Jayne shot upright. "You *what?*"

"They aren't on the usual quarterly system."

"Because their income is seasonal and they run on a different fiscal year. They only operate during the fall Renaissance Festival." Bill would have known that if he'd been looking after their accounts the way he claimed he'd been doing.

"Okay, so what do I do now?"

You're an executive accountant. You should know. Jayne thought a moment. There would be penalties and interest. "Bill, I honestly don't know."

"Don't give me that!"

"I don't! I've never missed a filing deadline. We'll have to ask Mr. Waterman what the procedures are for paying the penalties. I'm assuming the client wouldn't be billed for them."

"You set me up. You did this on purpose to make me look bad."

Jayne rolled her eyes. "I've been too busy to take time to make you look bad. I suggest you approach Mr. Waterman, or if you wait, I can talk to him for you. Right now, I have more calls to return."

"I'll talk to Waterman myself." Bill slammed the phone in her ear.

So he was mad. She was mad, too. Maybe now he wouldn't be so cocky.

After taking a few calming breaths, Jayne called the clients next. Both had tried to reach Bill and he hadn't returned their calls. Jayne answered their questions, relying on memory since she didn't have their records with her, told them she'd verify figures and hung up the phone.

Bill Pellman an executive accountant? Ha. She almost felt sorry that he'd have to confess a whopper of a mistake on his first day in his new position. Almost.

Jayne was just stuffing her purse into the bottom file cabinet drawer when the door to her office opened and Sylvia, carrying three coffees and a white bakery bag that was larger than usual, came dragging in.

"Sylvia!"

Sylvia wore the same outfit she'd had on yesterday, her eye makeup was smudged and her hair had lost half its volume. And she'd come in to work that way?

She flopped onto the couch. "I'm in love."

"With Sandor?"

"Who else?"

"Well, I wouldn't know since I haven't seen you since you left with him yesterday."

"Isn't he the most…" She sighed and trailed off, her eyes closing.

"Sylvia!"

She yawned, then sat up and dug in the bag. "We stayed out all night. I'm exhausted and famished." Pulling out a large pastry, she bit into it, then peeled off the plastic cover from one of the cups and drank half the contents before Jayne could walk across the room.

"Sausage kolaches?" Jayne peered into the bag and found two more. "I thought we were dieting for the cruise."

"But I'm starving!" Sylvia drained the cup, then started in on the second.

Jayne reached for the last coffee before Sylvia drank that one, too.

"I think I might live now." She popped the last

bite of kolache into her mouth and held out the bag to Jayne. "Want one?"

Jayne started to take it, then shook her head. "You go ahead. I had a huge dinner last night." She waited for Sylvia to ask her about dinner, but Sylvia's head was full of Sandor.

"I had so much fun! He knows *everybody*. We went to so many clubs, I lost count." She bit into her second kolache, wolfing it down as fast as she had the first. "We were with all these models and actors, except the crowd kept changing as we went from place to place."

"And you did this all night?"

Sylvia nodded. "And all yesterday afternoon, too. I went to lunch with Sasha and Sandor and a couple of others at the Mucky Duck—except that they didn't eat more than a few bites, so I didn't, either. I mean, I felt like such a pig. Then we heard this group rehearse, they told us about another place, so we went there and kind of kept going."

"What about your job?"

She made a face. "I called in sick."

"The way you look today, they'll believe you."

"Oh, come on, Jayne. Just because you never have any fun—"

"I have fun. In fact—"

But Sylvia didn't hear her. "—doesn't mean you should spoil mine. I met this great guy and I went for it. You can hardly blame me."

Jayne didn't blame her, but she remembered Garrett's words. "He's a love 'em and leave 'em type. Be careful."

"How do you know?"

"Garrett told me."

"Well, Sandor says Garrett is a looking-for-the-perfect-woman-type and no one ever measures up."

"You talked about Garrett?" Jayne edged closer to the sofa, Bill and his problems forgotten.

Sylvia finished the second kolache and eyed the last one in the bag. "Talked about you, too."

Jayne groaned. "I know. They could hardly *wait* to get out of here yesterday."

"I don't know about that, *buuuut...*"

Sylvia drew out the word until Jayne burst out with, "But what?"

"Well, both Sandor and Sasha say Garrett talks about you all the time."

"He does?" Jayne couldn't stop her pleased smile, even though she knew Sylvia would see it.

And she did, nodding with satisfaction. "According to Garrett, you're the only reason they still have the company."

Business hype to reassure his family. Jayne's smile faded. "That's not true. He just told them that to convince them to listen to what I had to say. In fact, I still don't think they realize how serious things—" At the last moment, she realized that she was talking to Sylvia who wasn't supposed to know about the agency's business.

"Sandor told me their manager ran off with all their money."

"I guess they do understand," Jayne murmured.

"Yeah, they're pretty bummed. But Garrett does talk about you," she added slyly.

Jayne stood and carried her coffee over to her desk.

"We've put in some pretty long hours together lately."

"Including last night at Nicky V's?"

Jayne whirled back around. "How did you know?"

"We ran into that Micky girl from the agency at one of the clubs and she said she'd seen you with Garrett. And you didn't even tell me!"

"How could I? You weren't around! Oh, and I wanted you to go shopping with me—"

"You went shopping and I missed it?"

"I had to. I bought a black suit," Jayne told her.

Sylvia groaned and slapped her hand to her forehead. "Jayne, we've got to get you out of suits!"

"I felt comfortable in it," Jayne said defensively.

"You're supposed to be sexy, not comfortable."

"Can't I be both?"

"It hardly ever works that way." Sylvia slipped off her shoe and rubbed her foot. "Blisters," she said and grimaced. "So what kind of evening was it? And more important, did he kiss you good-night?"

"I…" Jayne had dreamed about the kiss last night. But was she dreaming about a dream, or had it really happened? "On the forehead for sure."

Sylvia blinked at her. "What does that mean?"

"It means I blanked out anything else."

"Oh, this is great." Sylvia laughed and clapped her hands. "He kissed you senseless."

Had he?

"So when are you going out with him again?"

Jayne stared at her coffee. "He didn't say anything about going out again."

"He will."

"I don't know, Sylvia. I'm me and he's..." She gestured wildly. "You know."

"No, I don't know."

Jayne sighed. "Even if...you ought to see the way women look at him!"

"Well, yeah. The man is a serious hunk!"

"I'd have to compete with them." She shrugged. "I can't."

"Not if you don't try."

"What do you mean?"

"Well, you know how we're dieting for the cruise? We'll do more. New makeup, new clothes. Gosh, you spend half your time over there in the middle of model central, you ought to pick up some tips."

Jayne thought seriously about what Sylvia had said. Would it hurt to wear just a touch of makeup? And must her suits be blue or gray or black? Did she always have to wear white shirts with little scarf ties? She'd already mostly given up her ten o'clock chocolate doughnut, maybe if she'd cut back more, she'd drop a few pounds and discover she had cheekbones, too.

And then, if she became thin enough and beautiful enough, she'd be good enough for Garrett.

"Okay, let's do it!"

"All right!" Sylvia jumped up. "And the first thing we're going to do is get rid of these." She stepped over the coffee table and untied Jayne's striped ribbon tie.

"Hey!"

"Live a little. Unbutton a button."

Feeling reckless, Jayne did just that.

She and Sylvia were grinning at each other when Jayne's intercom buzzed.

It was Mr. Waterman's secretary. "Jayne, he wants to see you." She lowered her voice. "Pronto."

"I've got to go," Jayne said.

Sylvia was already leaving. "Me, too. Bye!"

What could Mr. Waterman want now? Without taking time to retie her tie, Jayne jogged down the hallway, taking two deep recovery breaths before opening Mr. Waterman's door.

Bill was with him, looking innocent. Angelic, even.

Jayne knew that was a bad sign.

Mr. Waterman's gaze swept over her, lingering at her throat. "Jayne, Bill has brought a very serious matter to my attention."

That would be the missed deadlines, Jayne guessed, except that Bill didn't look cowed.

"You've missed two filing deadlines."

Jayne was so stunned, she literally opened and closed her mouth. "These were clients you assigned to Bill while I had to work over at Venus."

"But you should have alerted him to the upcoming deadlines, therefore, I'm holding you responsible."

"If Bill had read the timetable in the front of each file, he would have seen the upcoming deadlines for himself."

"Jayne." Mr. Waterman looked disappointed. "It isn't like you to try to shift the blame."

"Mr. Waterman, I have never missed a filing deadline and I wouldn't have missed this one, but it was Bill's responsibility." *The same Bill you just promoted because he'd handled my accounts so well*, she wanted to add.

Shaking his head, Mr. Waterman took a gold pen from the set on his desk. "I'm going to have to note this in your record."

Unbelievable. "Then I suggest you also make a note of my strong protest." And for the first time since she'd gone to work for Pace Waterman, Jayne left Mr. Waterman's office without being dismissed first.

And she wasn't going to hang around and watch Bill gloat, either. Gathering up the records she hadn't yet started to work on, Jayne headed back over to Venus, Inc., crowd of tall, skinny women or not.

Garrett leaned over the counter and looked at the messages Micky had collected for him.

Jayne hadn't returned his call.

It was the kiss, Garrett had no doubt. A really great good-night kiss after a long evening seemed like a good idea at the time, but Jayne had probably thought about it and felt awkward this morning.

He didn't want her feeling awkward. He'd made progress with her yesterday and he didn't want to go backward.

"Garrett, what do you think?"

His mother had brought him three applications and was waiting for his comments.

"They're blondes," he said.

"Yes, you know Gustav wants blondes to show his fall line."

Garrett studied the instant photos that had been taken in the studio this morning. Then he looked at his mother.

"Oh, I know." She took the applications back from

him. "We couldn't send Gustav three green girls anyway. But Garrett, your Jayne said we needed to sign more models and there weren't any suitable candidates today."

"We'll have to advertise."

"Of course we'll have to advertise!"

"I mean seriously advertise and that's expensive. What do you think about sponsoring a contest?"

Rebecca closed her eyes and shuddered. "I hate those. So much work."

"Hate what?" Sasha came over with the rest of the applications, looked at the three her mother held, rolled her eyes and took the papers, which she stuck in a large envelope with the date on it.

"Modeling contests," her mother said.

"Ooh, me, too. You know what? I think we ought to go poaching."

"He who lives by poaching, dies by poaching," Garrett said. The last thing he wanted was to alienate the other agencies by stealing their models.

"It was just a thought," Sasha said. "Ask Jayne what she thinks."

"Ask Jayne what she thinks about what?" She stood in the doorway with an armload of files. Garrett looked even better this morning than he had last night. She clutched the files closer to her as she walked into the reception area. It was a good thing his mother and sister were there. Between Sylvia's pep talk and Bill's treachery, Jayne was in a strange mood. Who knew what she might do?

"I didn't think you were going to be over here until

this afternoon,'' Garrett said with a wide smile. He looked pleased to see her.

"Neither did I. So what did you want to ask me?"

"Sasha wants to steal models from other agencies."

Sasha made a thumbs-up sign.

Jayne laughed. "Can you do that?"

"It's not something I'd want to do on a large scale."

"We'd have to cut our agency percentage," Sasha said. "That'll get them to sign. Can you figure out how much we can cut and still make the money we need?" she asked Jayne.

"Are we talking a big cut?"

"Depends on how fast we want to grow our list."

"Sure," she said. "I can calculate some reduced percentages."

Garrett's mother spoke. "I don't like the idea except as an extreme measure. The other models always find out and then you have *them* signing with another agency and we'll end up worse than when we started."

"Then we'll have to offer them something else," Sasha said.

"Any ideas?" Garrett asked.

Micky had been silently eavesdropping. "Offer them Jayne."

"What?" Jayne heard herself echoed by the others.

Micky held up two sheets of paper. "Sasha showed me her binder and the way you broke down the expenses and income. It makes everything so clear and easy to understand. So I thought I'd copy the form and pretend I was a company."

"You're making a budget," Jayne said.

"Yeah, I guess so." Micky nodded. "I want to know where my money goes and save some for a new car, too. But nobody ever taught me how to handle money. I've just been happy if I had some left over at the end of the month. And after I got the form filled in, I was going to ask Jayne for help with it."

"And if it worked for Micky, I was going to do it, too," Sasha added.

"You know, they've got a point." Garrett looked approvingly at Micky. "Some of these girls start making all this money and they don't know what to do with it, so they blow it all. If they sign with us, we could offer them Jayne's services as a financial counselor."

"Now, I approve of that idea," Rebecca said. "James and I have watched too many young women self-destruct in this business. And it is a business, which they seem to forget."

"Except I'm more of an accountant than a financial planner," Jayne felt compelled to point out.

"But you could do it, couldn't you?" Garrett asked.

Of course, she could do it. "Yes, but I'd want to work with an investment banker I trust."

"I don't have a problem with that." He looked at the others and they shook their heads. Turning to her, he asked, "So what do you say?"

"It sounds great, except that you're looking at a lot of accounting hours and I don't know if Venus can afford to keep paying the Pace Waterman rates as it is. It would be cheaper to hire your own business manager."

Garrett smiled. "The job is yours, if you want it."

CHAPTER EIGHT

JAYNE stared at him. Working here? All the time? Seeing Garrett *every day?*

Jayne's future lay in two paths before her. If she followed the Pace Waterman path, she'd be traveling a familiar road that had lately developed potholes. The Venus way was risky. They were still on shaky financial footing and she had no idea where the job would lead.

But she'd really enjoy the journey.

Garrett widened his smile persuasively, showing his dimples on purpose, she knew.

"Are you offering me the position of business manager of Venus, Inc.?"

"Yes," he answered without hesitation.

"Okay," she accepted, also without hesitation.

Garrett blinked at the easy victory. "Are you sure?"

Was she? Jayne never made impulsive decisions and this was about as impulsive as they got. She'd been with Pace Waterman her entire working career.

And if she stayed there much longer, she'd probably end up working for Bill Pellman. "I'm sure," she said firmly.

"Yea!" Micky cheered.

"Mom, you and I are gonna go get us some models." Sasha tossed the envelope with the day's applications onto Micky's counter, and linked arms with her mother.

Rebecca Charles looked thoughtful. "Your father and I heard from Gustav that both Brynn Francis and Darnia Vanderhoff are unhappy with their representation."

Sasha looked at her in surprise. "You've got gossip and you didn't share?"

"At the time it didn't seem important," Rebecca said as they left the room.

Garrett had been studying Jayne. "Let's talk." He took the files from her and gestured for her to follow him. He led the way to George Windom's former office.

"Surprised you, didn't I?" she asked when they were inside.

"Yes." He stacked the files on the credenza. "But I've discovered several surprising things about you lately." He leaned against the desk and scorched her with a look.

The suddenness of it stole her breath.

Now is a good time to take me in your arms, Jayne thought.

And it was a lovely thought, except for the fact that he'd just become her boss and they were at the company in full view of anyone walking by—including his mother, for Pete's sake.

"I enjoyed last night," he murmured.

"Me, too," she admitted shyly.

He hesitated then said, "You do know that's not why I offered you the position here."

"You do know that's not why I accepted the position here," she shot back.

"Good." His smile crinkled the corners of his eyes. "Still, you can take more time to decide before you quit your job."

Jayne didn't want more time. "Have you changed your mind about hiring me?"

"No."

"Then I hope you aren't going to try to talk me out of this."

"No way. I've wanted to hire you since the beginning, but I didn't think we had a chance. Pace Waterman is a prestigious firm."

"And you're wondering why I'd give that up."

"In a word, yes."

Jayne looked at him and knew she couldn't admit that her decision was based in part by a desire to be near him. She wasn't even ready to admit that to herself. "They're an old, staid, conservative firm. And I was becoming old and staid right along with them. I've been...restless, I guess you could say. I couldn't figure out what was wrong and then yesterday..." She could still see Bill's smug face and Mr. Waterman's expression this morning as he blamed her for Bill's mistake. She squared her shoulders. "I realized that I've gone as far as I can go with that company. I'm ready for a change."

"I hope you're ready for a challenge."

"That, too." She should be impulsive more often. It felt good. "Shall we talk terms?"

"Yes, I guess you would want to know your salary." He laughed and rubbed the back of his neck. "How about paying yourself what we were paying Pace Waterman?"

Jayne laughed. "Very generous. You can't afford that."

"Then split the difference. Can we afford that?"

She knew it would be less than the salary George Windom had drawn, yet it was a substantial increase over her current salary. "Yes, with me working for you, you can."

"So, are we all set?"

"Let's see, I've already analyzed your benefits package, so I'm familiar with that...what's my title going to be?"

Garrett spread his hands. "Whatever you want."

Jayne looked around the plush office. "Goddess has a nice ring to it."

Garrett laughed. "All right, accounting goddess, when can you start?"

Giving two weeks notice to Mr. Waterman was almost as satisfying as showing Bill the workload he'd inherit.

Mr. Waterman was genuinely surprised at her resignation. He didn't try to persuade her to stay, which was disappointing, but watching Bill's face drain of color completely made up for it.

"When—when did you get all this done?" he asked as she showed him her client files.

"Oh, I put in a lot of evenings and weekends," Jayne said cheerfully. But she wasn't giving Pace Waterman free overtime any longer.

Only Sylvia was despondent over her leaving, but brightened when she realized visiting Jayne meant seeing Sandor, if he was in town.

But the Charleses, with the exception of Garrett,

had gone to New York and elsewhere to talk with models. Garrett was swamped with work. He and Jayne barely saw each other.

Jayne didn't mind, in fact she preferred it—for now. As part of their self-improvement campaign, she and Sylvia had joined a health club, though how someplace that made a person feel so bad could be called a *health* club escaped Jayne.

When she tried to get out of bed the first morning after her complimentary session with the fitness trainer, her stomach muscles screamed and she joined them. It was worse when she ate her breakfast of half a grapefruit and dry toast. The food lasted about thirty minutes, then she was hungry again. Then her stomach hurt both inside and out.

The second session was devoted to a cardio workout, which made a new set of muscles sore before the old ones had calmed down.

"Just by hanging around Sandor before he left, I've lost five pounds!" announced Sylvia when she came by at ten o'clock several mornings later. "Think how much I'll lose when he gets back!"

Jayne's stomach growled at the sight of the white bag she carried. Sylvia set a cup on her desk, opened the bag and tossed her a plum.

Jayne caught it. "Oh, goodie. I was just thinking of how hungry I was and how much I wanted a *plum.*"

"We have to be strong for each other," Sylvia told her and virtuously bit into her own plum.

Jayne took the lid off her cup. There was a pale amber liquid inside. "What happened to the coffee?"

"That's herbal tea. It's better for you."

Jayne put her head on her desk and whimpered.

By the end of the week, Sylvia had lost seven pounds and Jayne had lost half a pound, but only if she stood on the edge of her scales.

"Don't worry about it. I'm taller and it's probably all water weight," Sylvia consoled her when they met at the gym.

"I wouldn't mind losing water weight," Jayne grumbled and stepped on the treadmill.

"Or, I know. You're building muscle. Muscle weighs more than fat."

"You mean I might *gain* weight going through all this torture?" Jayne wailed.

"Garrett, in addition to Brynn and Darnia, we've found several rising stars who are interested in signing with us." Garrett's father read their names. His mother was on the extension phone and added comments about each.

"If you think they're worth signing, then go ahead," he said. After so many years in the business, his parents could instantly tell whether a model had potential or not.

"We think you should come here and talk to the girls. They're nervous about being represented by an agency based outside New York," his father said.

This was a perception problem they'd had before. "You did tell them that *they* don't have to leave New York?"

His mother spoke. "Yes, but it would be best if you reassured them in person. It would also give you a chance to explain Jayne's services."

"You know I'd fly up if I could, but right now isn't a good time."

"Jayne starts on Monday, doesn't she?" his mother asked.

"That's why now isn't a good time."

"She seems very capable of running things in your absence."

"Mom, she can't book models."

"I don't expect her to."

"It's only for a few days, Garrett," his father added.

Garrett closed his eyes. The dinner he'd had with Jayne seemed a very long time ago—because it *had* been a very long time ago. And now he was supposed to leave on her first day at the agency? Apparently so. "I'll see you Monday afternoon," he told his parents.

Jayne had bought a new outfit for her first day at Venus, Inc. Unfortunately she didn't get to buy it in a smaller size.

And, in spite of Sylvia's protests, it was a suit. But it was a suit in pale blue, which was a start. It had a flat knit shell in the same shade, which left Jayne's neck bare, so she bought a heavy gold choker and matching earrings to wear. She'd even experimented with a little blush and mascara and was spending lunch—or what passed for her lunch these days—with Micky. They were trading makeup tips for Jayne with budget help for Micky.

As soon as she walked through the door, Micky beamed at her. "Oh, go look at your office!" She came out from behind the high reception desk. "I want to watch."

With Micky following her, Jayne turned the corner in time to see Garrett fastening a brass name plaque to her door.

Jayne felt a thrill go through her. Her new position was official. "Garrett, thanks. That's so—"

Grinning, he'd stepped back and she read the plaque:

Jayne Nelson
Accounting Goddess

"Garrett!"

"Isn't that the title you said you wanted?"

Jayne laughed. "Well, yes, but I can't believe you actually put it on a sign!"

"Isn't that great?" Giggling, Micky practically danced her way back to the reception area.

Garrett opened the door and gestured Jayne inside.

A large sophisticated arrangement of tropical flowers sat on the desk. Pleased, she read the card, already guessing that they were from Garrett.

"Welcome to Venus from the Charles family," read the card and Jayne felt a prick of disappointment that Garrett hadn't written something more personal.

He made up for it a moment later.

"I'm very glad you're here," he said in a low voice that made her shiver. "I'd intended to take you to lunch today as a celebration, but we'll have to postpone it. I've got to catch a plane to New York."

New York? He was leaving? On her first day? *Be professional, Jayne.* "That's okay. Micky and I had made plans for lunch.'' She was pleased with the casual tone in her voice.

Maybe it was too casual.

Disappointment crossed Garrett's face. ''Oh. Good.'' He seemed at a loss for words. ''Well, I know it's rotten to leave you on your first day, but I've got a noon flight.''

Jayne forced herself to smile. ''It's not like I've never been here before. Don't worry about me. Have a safe trip.''

It was probably just as well that the entire Charles family was out of the office while Jayne settled in.

It seemed she was spending more and more time on the telephone, closing accounts, trying to reassure creditors and talking with Elaine, her contact at the bank.

And then there was the news that George Windom's trail had led south, out of the country. Jayne wasn't surprised. She had a frank chat with the investigators about the chances of recovering any of the funds he'd stolen. They weren't encouraging, which didn't surprise her, either.

Reluctantly she called the Charles apartment in New York, hoping to get Garrett.

Sandor answered. ''Yo.''

There was no reason to ask for Garrett. She was only relaying information. ''Sandor, this is Jayne Nelson.''

''What's up?''

''I was just calling to let you know that the investigators have determined that George Windom has left the country.''

"I could have told them that."

Privately Jayne agreed. "Now it's been confirmed."

"Whatever. Say, what's the deal with this allowance you've got us on?"

"Allowance?"

"Yeah. Where's my money?"

"George took most of it."

"No. I mean the money for the shoot Sasha and I did for the perfume."

"As I explained in the new business plan, you and your family are going to have to put as much of your income as possible back into the company."

"Man, I got like, a third of what I should."

And it was still a lot of money. "I know it's going to be hard and you're going to have to make sacrifices—"

"I can't live on that!"

"Well, Sandor, you're just going to have to cut back for a while."

"Forget it!" He slammed the phone in her ear.

Jayne was getting tired of having angry young men hang up on her, but she refused to tattle to Garrett.

Until three days later when Elaine called from the bank. "Jayne, I'm sorry I didn't catch this in time to alert you, but there's been a check returned for insufficient funds on Alexander Charles's personal account."

"Sandor has bounced a check?"

"Three thousand dollars."

"*What?*"

"Do you want to transfer funds from another account to cover it?"

"No. Let me consult with them before we do anything."

Elaine hesitated and Jayne knew she'd already asked her to bend the rules more than she should have.

Elaine exhaled. "Just a couple of hours, okay?"

"Thanks."

Jayne called Garrett. He wasn't at the apartment, so she left a message on the answering machine.

"I have a feeling this isn't good news," he said when he returned her call.

Jayne told him about the check. "If you want to transfer funds from somewhere to cover it, let me know right now so I can call Elaine at the bank."

Garrett swore softly. "Any other time and I'd let Sandor deal with the consequences, but right now, we need to look rock solid financially or our creditors will get nervous, especially after that last round of bounced checks."

Garrett was quiet for a moment and Jayne let him think. "Transfer his percentage from the operating fund and be sure you charge it against him," he finally instructed.

"Will do."

Jayne would have liked to have chatted a bit longer, but knew she had to call Elaine at once.

Fortunately, she was in time, but shuffling expenses for the month took her the rest of the afternoon.

What a day. It was time to meet Sylvia at the gym. Jayne filled her briefcase with paperwork to read at home. She now had a key to the back entrance, so she walked down the hall intending to let Micky know she was leaving.

Micky was talking to someone as she filed her nails.

"...three calls from Patrick. Says you two would be perfect for this white wool in Alaska shoot. He wants to go all black-and-white and arty with snow."

"I hate snow."

Jayne stopped in surprise. That sounded like Sandor.

"He knows. Says he'll bump up your rates."

"And I need the money now that little plain Jayne has closed the coffers so to speak."

By now Jayne had figured out he was on the speak-erphone.

"Hey. I like her. She's smart."

Jayne smiled. Good old Micky. Intending to say good-night, Jayne continued walking down the hall-way.

"Darling, when you look the way she does you'd better hope you've got brains."

"Sandor, you're being so mean."

"Look, she whined to big brother and I had to lis-ten to a dreary lecture about the *family* pulling to-gether. Well Sasha and I are the main support of the *family*, so if I want to buy a new sound system, then I should be able to and not have to grovel to a frumpy little accountant."

One part of her, the mature, accountant part, knew Sandor was blowing off steam after being chewed out by Garrett.

The other part—the part that desperately wanted to be pretty—felt the sting of his words.

What had she done? Jayne numbly crept back down the hallway. Based on dinner and a good-night kiss, she'd given up an excellent position with a top accounting agency so she could fuel her fantasies about Garrett.

She'd been kidding herself. How could he find her attractive? She was frumpy, lumpy and short.

And then she saw the brass nameplate gleaming on her office door. *Accounting Goddess*. Garrett had put that there. The same Garrett who had never made her feel frumpy, lumpy, or short.

Jayne stared at the nameplate and was filled with new resolve. There was nothing she could do about being short, but she didn't have to stay frumpy and lumpy. She was working in a modeling agency, after all. She should look her best.

Garrett would want her to.

"Are you absolutely certain water doesn't have any calories?" Jayne complained at the end of another week of abusing her muscles and depriving herself of food. It was cardio day, so she and Sylvia were on the treadmills.

"Your metabolism hasn't reset itself yet, that's all," Sylvia said. "Don't you feel more energetic?"

"No," grumbled Jayne.

Sylvia felt more energetic. She told Jayne so repeatedly. Sylvia's already small skirts were slipping and sliding all around her now, too.

"Hey, Marlena said you canceled your facial."

"Yes." Jayne's voice was clipped. "What's the point?"

"Well...sometimes people get pimples after facials."

Jayne knew this, unfortunately. "I repeat—what's the point?"

"To have pretty skin."

"My skin looked better before."

Sylvia didn't contradict her, but she couldn't really. Jayne's face had been a mass of red bumps after both facials with the skin technician at the spa Micky said all the models loved.

"I don't enjoy it as much if you're not there. Why don't you see if Olga has room for a leg wax?"

"Yet another fun activity."

"Then go have a pedicure," Sylvia said with exasperation.

"There's a thought." Jayne liked pedicures, even though she was the only one who ever saw her toes. Sometimes, when she was in her office, she kicked off her shoes, just so she could look down at her toes. She wondered if Garrett liked toes.

"So when's Garrett get back?" Sylvia asked.

"He and his family are going to be in New York another week," Jayne answered.

She knew Sylvia was really wondering about Sandor, but didn't want to ask outright. He hadn't called her and in spite of what Garrett had said about Sylvia not getting hurt, Jayne was afraid that Sylvia had deeper feelings for Sandor than was wise. She knew better than to say anything against him, however much she might want to.

"More time to lose weight!" With that, Sylvia increased the incline on the treadmill.

"You're dropping weight pretty fast, aren't you?"

"Twelve pounds, but I've really only cut out snacks. I never realized how much I ate in a day."

Jayne had lost a whopping two pounds and she felt she'd cut out as much food as Sylvia. Perhaps not.

But she'd made real progress on the makeup front. With Micky's help, she'd bought shadows and pencils, powders and creams, foundation and lipstick. She had to get up thirty minutes earlier in the morning just to put everything on.

Between that, the facials and various beauty treatments and the exercising, she was spending an additional two hours a day on nothing but her appearance.

She hoped Garrett would think it was worth it.

CHAPTER NINE

FRIDAY was a wonderful and glorious day. Garrett called to say that he and his parents were flying back that weekend.

And the skirt of Jayne's pale blue suit was too loose at the waist.

The waists of most of Jayne's skirts were loose. The only ones that fit were the ones that had been too snug in the first place.

She called Sylvia. "What do I do?"

"You pin it with a safety pin, then meet me for a long lunch and we'll shop."

Jayne skipped breakfast, even though she knew she was breaking a cardinal rule of dieting, because she was afraid to eat anything in case her sudden weight loss reversed itself.

Sylvia was impressed with Jayne's loose skirts. "It's like the fat finally got tired of hanging on and just let go." She flipped through the rack of dresses a size smaller than Jayne usually wore.

"It's been a month—isn't it about time?"

"I'd say so. Actually I thought you were just cheating on your diet."

"Sylvia!"

Sylvia pulled out a sleeveless turquoise sheath and held it up to Jayne.

"I can't wear that to the office."

148

"Sure you can. It comes with this." Sylvia hauled out a jacket with a jewel collar.

And Jayne fell in love. She fell in love with a lot of the clothes they found and spent way too much money. Buying clothes had never been so much fun.

"You know something?" Sylvia studied her in the dressing room mirror. "Your face is thinner."

"Good."

"Well...your hair doesn't look right anymore."

"My hair hasn't looked right since the perm." Jayne fluffed it, then pulled it back. "What do you think?"

"I'm thinking haircut."

Jayne was trying to find a diplomatic way to keep Sylvia's scissors out of her hair when she said, "Ask Micky who cuts her hair and if you can be worked in on Saturday. Stress that it's an emergency."

On Monday morning, Garrett knocked on the door of his accounting goddess and found a stranger sitting at her desk.

"Garrett! You're back."

"Jayne?" The woman sounded like Jayne, but didn't look like the Jayne he'd left two weeks ago. What had she done to herself? "You...look great," he said, knowing a comment was called for.

Beaming, Jayne announced, "I cut my hair."

Garrett studied her. The new length was only a couple of inches shorter, but her curls were now glazed into even corkscrews that fell just below her cheeks. It put her face into proportion and emphasized her eyes. "I like it."

Garrett peered closer, noting the addition of

makeup and a professional eyebrow shaping as well. She looked like Jayne, but with more polish.

He decided he could get used to her new appearance. "I like the rest of you, as well," he said, indicating her outfit with a sweep of his hand. "So how about that lunch I owe you? Can you make it today?" After two undiluted weeks with his family, he was ready to talk about something other than clothes and who wore them.

Her smile seemed brighter than he'd ever seen it. "I'd love to!"

As the morning wore on, Garrett looked forward to lunch with Jayne as an oasis of calm in the midst of the frantic activity that had exploded in the agency since his return.

Several of the new models they'd signed planned to visit and make the rounds in Houston—and talk with Jayne, as they'd been promised. Garrett knew that she'd be overloaded within a few days and wanted to have this time with her before they both got too busy.

He took Jayne to an Italian place he'd recently discovered. Small, tucked behind stately oaks on lower Westheimer, it wasn't popular with the "in" crowd yet. Garrett was counting on a peaceful meal during which he and Jayne could continue their conversation from the dinner they'd shared. He wanted to clear his mind of the modeling business and Jayne was the only person he knew who could do that.

As he suspected, only two other tables were occupied. A mural was slowly winding its way across the stucco walls. Garrett had enjoyed watching its progress on his previous visits.

"This place has great manicotti," he suggested when they opened their menus. "Or if you're feeling self-indulgent, there's always fettuccine Alfredo."

"With about a million fat grams," Jayne said, shaking her head. "And the manicotti isn't much better."

She couldn't know that she sounded exactly like his mother and sister and half the models he knew. He hadn't expected Jayne to care about fat grams, or if she did, he didn't want to know about it. "Well, whatever you order, save room for the tiramisu. It's some of the best I've ever had."

"Too rich." Jayne handed the menu to the waiter. "I'll have the fruit plate without dressing, please."

The waiter wrote and raised his eyebrow inquiringly.

"Nothing else, thanks," Jayne said.

Garrett laughed. "That's a joke, right? Now what are you really having?"

"The fruit plate," she insisted, a determined expression on her face.

Feeling vaguely disappointed, Garrett ordered the manicotti. "So how have you been getting along at the agency while I've been gone?" he asked.

"Fine," she answered. "It was probably the easiest transition in the history of job changes."

"Any other fallout from George?"

Jayne shook her head. "I've got everything under control."

Garrett wanted more detail, but supposed it wasn't fair to ask her when she didn't have the records nearby for reference. "Payroll's coming up. How do things look?"

"Even with covering Sandor's check, you'll still be okay."

Garrett surmised he was going to have to wait for a definition of "okay." It seemed Jayne didn't want to get into an in-depth business discussion, which should have been fine. He hadn't intended this to be a strictly business lunch, anyway. It was just that she was usually very precise in her answers and he enjoyed listening to that precision.

"How was New York?" she asked. "Any good gossip?"

Garrett thought he'd never hear Jayne utter the word "gossip." "Political, or financial?"

She laughed. "Fashion, of course."

Jayne hadn't been idle while Garrett had been gone. Instead of taking home financial journals to read, she'd been reading the fashion magazines in the reception area. She wanted to impress Garrett with her new knowledge of his business. It only made sense, since it was now her business, too.

As she talked, she noticed that he was looking at her in a way he never had before. Good. She wanted him seeing her in a different way. She had to have *some* reason to force herself to the gym every day.

She'd also made it a point to learn the models they currently represented and to identify the stars who were signed with competing agencies. He probably thought she wasn't interested, and until recently, she hadn't been. "Tell me, did your parents get Brynn and Darnia to sign with us?"

"Ah." Garrett shifted in his chair. "They're thinking about it, but probably yes."

"That's great. I saw the editorial layout they did in the May issue of *Vogue*."

He looked at her in surprise. "You did?"

Jayne nodded, smiling in satisfaction. Garrett was impressed, she just knew it.

"You'll get to meet them later this week," he told her. "They want to talk to you about their personal finances."

"I'm going to meet *Brynn and Darnia?*"

Garrett eyed her warily. "Yes."

"Oh my gosh. What am I going to wear? I mean, I want to look professional, but not frumpy. After all, our business is fashion."

Garrett just stopped himself from putting his hands around the neck of the alien sitting at the table with him and shouting, "Who are you and what have you done with Jayne?"

He didn't but after half an hour of the sort of insipid conversation he'd hoped to avoid, he paid the bill, not even waiting to see if she wanted coffee. He didn't think he could stand it.

What had happened to her while he'd been gone? This afternoon, when he heard her report, would be better.

It had to be better.

"Sylvia, can you talk?" Jayne rarely called her friend during business hours, but just had to after the wonderful lunch she'd shared with Garrett.

"Yeah, I can type and listen at the same time. Was lunch good?"

"I didn't forget a single model's name *and* I even discussed a couple of designer trends!"

"Way to go!"

"You ought to see the way he's looking at me now. I think he's actually noticed me!"

She and Sylvia agreed to meet fifteen minutes earlier than usual at the gym and Jayne got ready for her meeting with Garrett.

About thirty minutes before she was expecting him, she was surprised when he knocked on the open door. "I wasn't—"

He held up a hand. "I'm early, I know. I wanted to get away from the phone." Sitting in one of the chairs by her desk, he exhaled and rubbed the side of his neck. "I feel like I've been talking for hours."

"A lot of work piled up while you were gone."

He made a face. "And I haven't done any of it. You know it's one thing to sign new models, but it's another to find work for them. I've had to promise Sasha and Sandor in return for getting some of these new girls booked."

Rubbing his shoulder, he added, "Signing new talent is great, but what we need are a couple of stars to attract attention to us. Brynn and Darnia are just about to make supermodel status. If we get them, our expansion will jump ahead of schedule and if we don't, word will get around about why we didn't and…" He trailed off with a tired gesture.

He didn't have to spell it out. The agency needed to be a certain size to support the office space and personnel—including Jayne.

"Anyway, let's just say their visit this week is *very*

important.'' He smiled at her. ''I'm counting on you.''

Jayne swallowed and gazed into his blue eyes. ''I won't let you down.''

The morning of Brynn and Darnia's visit, Jayne stepped on her scales and saw another three-pound loss, and she wasn't even standing on the edges.

She would have given back one of those pounds for another hour's sleep, but she needed to spend extra time on her hair and makeup today.

She'd gone shopping with Sylvia last night and had splurged on an outfit from one of the boutiques near the agency. Sylvia had had to talk her into the long-sleeved silky shirt in cream with a whimsical cigars-and-smoke-curls print, and a short tobacco brown skirt because Jayne didn't think it was an appropriate outfit for work. It was trendy, but Jayne felt funny without her customary jacket. Still, if ever there was a day to look trendy, this was it.

She came in the front door so she could see Micky's reaction.

It was immediate and gratifying. ''Jayne! Ooh, I've been waiting for that outfit to go on sale. Did it?''

Jayne shook her head.

''Oh, wow.'' Micky was silent a moment, then said virtuously, ''Well, it's not in my budget.''

''It's not in mine, either,'' Jayne confessed. ''I'm paying for it out of savings.''

''You bought it 'cause Brynn and Darnia are coming in today.''

Jayne nodded, still not convinced she should be without her customary suit.

"I just put on black." Micky was wearing a sleeveless turtleneck and short skirt. "That always works when you don't have anything else."

"I'll remember that," Jayne said as voices sounded at the glass doors behind them. "It's easier on the budget."

She and Micky exchanged smiles, then Jayne turned, seeing Garrett first and, for a split second, a reflection of herself, or rather the way she'd look if all her dreams came true.

For that one instant, Jayne was tall and so thin she could eat a dozen orders of fettuccine Alfredo and not notice it. Her hair was long and straight and shot with golden streaks. Her cheekbones cast shadows and her full lips kept her mouth in a sensual pout. Miles of leg extended below her skirt.

Then Garrett pushed the door open and her reflection and another woman entered the reception area.

Jayne's fantasy turned into a nightmare. No woman wanted to come face-to-face with someone attired in an identical outfit. It was a thousand times worse when the other woman was three feet taller and a hundred pounds thinner.

She should have just worn black, she thought as Garrett led the models closer. A black suit.

"Hey, another Scarcella admirer!" said the model in Jayne's outfit. Jayne recognized her as Brynn. "Don't you just love his stuff?"

Jayne nodded wordlessly and avoided Garrett's eyes.

"Oh, I know," said the other model, who would have to be Darnia. "I have maybe twenty of his shirts. I buy them for the buttons."

Jayne had liked the buttons, which were shaped like little gold cigars, herself.

Darnia cocked her hip to one side in a casual pose Jayne envied, but knew better than to copy. "You know that on the grandfather clock shirt I've got, the hands on the buttons actually move?"

"Really? Cool," Brynn said.

Garrett stopped the button discussion before Jayne had to embarrass herself by admitting that she hadn't known weird prints and matching buttons were a Scarcella trademark. Actually she hadn't even known who Scarcella was until she'd gone on her fashion magazine reading binge.

"Jayne." Garrett touched her lightly on the arm. "This is Brynn Francis and Darnia Vanderhoff." He turned to the models. "Jayne is our accounting goddess."

Jayne couldn't even muster a smile at the joke.

"You're the one everybody's talking about!" Brynn said, looking surprised, but pleased.

"I am?" Jayne asked.

Darnia nodded. "Sasha claims you're a numbers genius."

"Well, I—"

"She is," Micky chimed in. "She helped me with my budget and when we get paid Friday, I'm going to have money left over for the first time. I was just *wasting* so much. I couldn't believe it."

"And she doesn't get paid extra for saying that," Garrett joked.

Everyone laughed, and Jayne joined in, though she didn't feel like laughing.

What must Garrett be thinking of her? She'd made

a horrible faux pas. She didn't look anything like the accountant he'd hired. Who'd want to trust money to a woman who spent outrageous amounts on shirts with cigar buttons?

Apparently other women who spent outrageous amounts on clothes. "Well, I want to go first," Brynn said. "I can tell that Jayne and I are on the same wavelength."

Jayne managed a smile, determined to reassure Garrett by acting as accountantlike as possible. "My office is this way. I have a financial profile form that I'd like for you both to fill out. Until I study it, I can only give you an overview of how we might structure your finances." She risked a look at him and was disturbed to see a blankly stunned expression on his face. She was going to have some serious fence mending to do after meeting with the models.

"I also want you to know that I'm not an investment specialist, but I know of a couple I've worked with before. They both have young children so they freelance out of their homes."

"Sounds good to me," Brynn said.

Darnia nodded and followed Jayne to her office.

Garrett stood staring after them, barely aware of the gentle warble of the telephone and the other background noises in the agency. He heard laughter and guessed that they'd seen the name plaque on Jayne's door.

Jayne.

Jayne.

Garrett felt as if he'd had the wind knocked out of him. She was even more brilliant than he'd realized.

Knowing how crucial signing Darnia and Brynn were to the success of Venus's expansion, she'd studied them, then dressed in their favorite designer. It had been pure serendipity that she and Brynn had been dressed alike, but not that they were wearing the same designer. That had been because Jayne had done her homework.

The two models had immediately accepted her and Garrett knew without a doubt that if they signed with his agency, no, *when* they signed, it would be because of Jayne.

He'd horribly misjudged her at lunch the other day and instead of helping her learn more about the fashion industry, he'd barely responded to her conversation. Of *course* she'd want to hear the latest news, since that's what Brynn and Darnia would know. She could talk to them about their world, then draw them into hers.

George Windom could never have accomplished that. He'd done them a favor by leaving and as far as Garrett was concerned, he could keep the money as long as he didn't come back. The painting he'd left behind was worth nearly as much as he'd embezzled and Garrett figured George knew it.

"Garrett? Do you need something?" Micky eyed him curiously.

"No...I..." *I need someone. Jayne.*

It was a defining moment. Micky's question wasn't supposed to be profound, but it crystallized Garrett's feelings. In that moment, he knew that Jayne was the woman for him.

He'd managed to find the one woman whom he could talk to about anything, a woman who could bridge both worlds the way he did, a woman who could talk fashion when she had to and finance when she needed to.

The woman he could imagine spending the rest of his life with.

"Garrett?" Micky looked concerned. "You aren't worried about Jayne, are you?"

"No." He smiled—grinned actually. "Jayne is…a goddess."

"I am just so jazzed about all this," Darnia said as Jayne saw her to the door. "Thanks, Jayne!" She waggled her fingers and strutted off down the hall.

Jayne closed her door and leaned her head against it. She'd only eaten half a piece of toast and three strawberries for breakfast. She thought her meeting with Darnia and Brynn had gone well, but she was feeling a little light-headed after three hours of number crunching.

She turned around to go back to her desk and see if she'd hidden any contraband food in it when she spotted Darnia's leather portfolio still propped on the floor against the desk. She grabbed it and hurried down the hall to catch her.

"I know, I liked her, too. And she doesn't look anything close to the way Sandor described her." Brynn was speaking.

Jayne slid to a halt, guessing who Sandor had been describing.

"I mean, she's wearing the same thing I am. I hardly call Scarcella hideous fashion."

"I don't know what his problem is," Micky said,

and Jayne figured they were all standing by the receptionist's desk.

"He can be such a jerk sometimes," Darnia agreed. "I can't believe he's Garrett's brother."

Jayne went back to her office. She'd return the portfolio in a few minutes.

She wasn't particularly upset about Sandor saying unflattering things about her—she'd already known she wasn't among his favorite people at the moment. But Darnia and Brynn hadn't said anything about her accounting abilities, only the way she looked.

She was still leaning against the edge of her desk thinking about what she'd heard when Garrett appeared in the doorway. He stood there for a moment just looking at her, then advanced purposefully into the room.

"You're incredible," he said when he stopped right in front of her. "All that talk about clothes and models...you knew how important it was for Brynn and Darnia to sign with us. Well, they just signed and it was all due to you."

Then he lowered his head and kissed her full on the lips. Right in her office. Just the way she'd fantasized. He filled his kiss with all the tenderness and restrained passion she could have wished for.

So where was her answering passion? Why wasn't she ecstatically happy?

Why wasn't she kissing him back?

That must be the reason. Jayne linked her arms around his neck and tried to recapture the magic of their kiss in the parking lot.

She remembered it now, in vivid detail, remembered the feel of his arms, the taste of his mouth and...

It wasn't the same.

She wanted it to be the same. Desperately.

"Jayne," he murmured as though he'd found her after a long search. "I don't know what I would have done without you."

He kissed her once more, hard and quick, before bending to pick up the portfolio. "Darnia forgot this and I'm supposed to be retrieving it."

"Oh, I...Garrett..."

He touched a finger to her lips. "We'll talk later."

Later turned into days later. Once word got out that Darnia and Brynn had left their old agency to sign with Venus, Garrett was inundated with inquiries.

Jayne found herself meeting with a steady stream of models. Not all of them signed with the agency, but she developed a fifteen-minute overview of what her services would be if the model signed with Venus, and it proved to be a successful sales tool.

Jayne, herself, spent more and more money on beauty treatments and clothes. She was beginning to resent the investment of time and money, but Garrett's attention made it all worthwhile.

Except...she didn't much like being judged on her appearance instead of her abilities. Even Sandor, who had returned with Garrett's family, accepted her financial strictures now when he hadn't before. As for working with the models, they could throw on a T-shirt and jeans and crawl out of bed looking better than Jayne did after two hours of primping each morning.

And today—today was the worst. Her weight hadn't budged since her meeting with Brynn and Darnia. Jayne was hungry and cranky and then Sylvia had come to visit.

Actually, Jayne knew she'd come to see why Sandor hadn't called her, but the reason didn't matter. Jayne was glad to see her anyway.

Until she went out to the reception area to meet Sylvia and saw her talking with Micky. In the background, were modeling hopefuls gathered for the Thursday open house screening.

Sylvia, newly slender and with her hair in a short spiky cut, looked exactly like one of them.

Jayne would never look exactly like one of them, and knew it, but the reality hit home in a way it hadn't before.

Her inner cry of anguish was drowned out by her stomach growling.

And things went downhill from there.

"Jayne!" she heard Garrett call for her.

"I'm out by Micky's desk," she answered.

Garrett came into the reception area looking enormously pleased. "Guess what?"

Jayne shook her head and to her surprise, Garrett grabbed her by the waist and twirled her around in front of everyone. "We've been asked to sponsor a modeling contest!"

"I thought you hated modeling contests," Jayne said, trying to regain her balance after he set her back down.

"They can be a pain, but the Houston Fashion Council is supplying the clothes. We'll run just the contest and fashion show part. The publicity will be phenomenal!''

"Oh, wow," Micky said. "Can I enter?"

Garrett seemed to remember where he was, but he still kept an arm around Jayne.

She was glad Sylvia was there to see it.

Garrett nodded a hello to her, then answered Micky's question. "It's a 'new faces' type of contest. First prize will be a contract with us, of course." He leveled a look at Micky. "You already have one."

She looked wistful, but didn't say anything more.

Garrett then said casually to Sylvia, "You should think about entering."

Sylvia?

Sylvia shared her surprise. "Me?"

"Yes. You've got that Russian gamine look that's going to be hot next season."

"Russian gamine?" Sylvia looked far too pleased.

Jayne tried to smile and managed one, not that anyone was looking at her.

"Yes, the way your eyes tilt at the corners and the dark hair."

Jayne's own eyes widened. Except for her eyes, Sylvia suddenly looked a lot like *Sasha.*

"I'm not too old?" she asked.

"For print work, perhaps, but there's a lot of local runway work. Think about it," Garrett advised.

"Well, yeah, sure. What do I do?"

"Fill out an entry form, which we don't have yet. Micky, would you make a note…?" Garrett smiled down at Jayne. "Things are going to get crazy around here."

"I thought they already were," she said lightly.

''I mean *really* crazy.''

There was one thing he wouldn't have to worry about, Jayne vowed. She may not be model material, but she was a darn good accountant.

It was time she started acting like one.

CHAPTER TEN

JAYNE didn't want to be a model, really she didn't. And she wasn't jealous of Sylvia, really she wasn't. It was just that she was feeling...left out.

Preparations for the modeling contest consumed every spare moment of everyone else's time, and much of that time was spent at the Galleria Hotel where the fashion show was being held. The contest was a Houston Fashion Council annual event, with only the sponsoring agency changing from year to year. Entry fees covered only part of the costs. Venus, Inc. was expected to cover the rest. And it was Jayne's job to figure out how they would manage that. So while the entire Charles family met with caterers, hotel event coordinators, modeling hopefuls, florists and printers, Jayne sat in lonely splendor in the plushly decorated office of her predecessor and performed triage on the bank account.

The numbers weren't hopeful, no matter how she added them up. She called her friend, Elaine, at the bank to sound her out about a loan. Elaine's voice had lost the friendliness it had held prior to Jayne asking her for so many favors. "Venus has no collateral. They don't meet acceptable risk criteria."

"They may not have concrete collateral, but the publicity from the contest will result in more bookings, which will generate more income," Jayne protested.

"Undercapitalization will doom their recovery." Elaine didn't even pretend to think it over. "Sorry, Jayne."

Jayne hung up the phone and held her head in her hands. If Elaine wouldn't even try, then there was no point in contacting anyone else. The phone rang while she sat there. Jayne stared at it—at the custom wood and brass telephone that George Windom had ordered for himself. She was tempted not to answer, since she suspected it was Garrett. She was right.

"Hi." His voice sounded tired. "Have you got those deposit checks ready for me yet?"

"Garrett..." Jayne exhaled, trying to find words to tell him he couldn't afford to sponsor the contest. For days she'd heard about what a fabulous opportunity the contest was and how good for business it was going to be. The expenses were already over budget.

"Aw, come on, Jayne." His voice was a rough whisper. "You can find the money for me, can't you?"

Jayne swiveled in her chair so she wouldn't have to look at the telephone. "Garrett, you can meet the payroll and pay the rent, or you can sponsor the contest."

"What about the entry fees?"

"Revenues from them aren't enough yet and you've had substantial printing and mailing costs, not to mention buying airplane tickets for the celebrity judges."

There was a silence. Jayne had been staring blankly. Now her eyes focused on the landscape above the credenza and she realized she hated a man she'd never met.

"I can't back out of the sponsorship now," Garrett insisted. "Think how that will look."

"Think how it will look when you can't pay your rent."

"You know...that might be better."

"Garrett—"

"Jayne, we're trying to establish ourselves as a major agency. Pulling out a week before the event will give us a reputation for unreliability at the very least. Gossip and rumor will do us in. But if we're late on the rent, the landlord isn't likely to call the wire services."

"Garrett—"

"Cut me a check for the hotel catering, the florist and the printer."

"Garrett, as your accountant, I must strongly advise against—"

"Don't argue with me. Do it."

He'd never spoken as harshly before, not even when they'd discovered George Windom's betrayal. To speak that way to her, after all she'd done, was more than Jayne could bear.

"I'll have the checks sent over by courier, since we're throwing money around."

"Fine." And with that clipped word, he hung up the telephone.

Tears blurred Jayne's vision. The colors of the painting, already fuzzy, smeared even more. She hated that painting and she wasn't going to look at it anymore. It was terrible enough that George had taken their money, but to leave the painting to mock them, when they couldn't sell it without court approval, was incredibly cruel. Jayne stalked over to it.

The frame was big and probably heavy. But she'd been working out. Her new muscles ought to be good for something. Reaching up, Jayne braced herself and carefully lifted the frame above the hanger in the wall, pulled the painting out a little bit, then lowered it to the floor.

Breathing a sigh of relief that she hadn't dropped it, she turned the picture toward the wall. Taped on the back was an envelope with Garrett's name on it. Jayne blinked back the traces of tears and stared at the envelope. Garrett couldn't have known that it was there. With fingers that shook a little, Jayne carefully peeled it away from the brown paper backing. She'd stared at enough of his handwriting to recognize the precise penmanship as George Windom's.

Desperately hoping the envelope contained good news, Jayne called the hotel and had Garrett paged, leaving her name with instructions to tell him it was urgent. After an eternity, she heard a familiar cheery voice. "Hey, Jayne!"

"Sylvia?"

"Yeah, it's me. Garrett can't talk to you right now, so I volunteered to get the message."

"Tell him it's really important that I speak with him."

"Jayne...he's right in the middle of some stuff."

Jayne closed her eyes and took two deep breaths. "Sylvia, shouldn't you be at work?"

"I'm meeting Sandor for lunch. What do you want me to tell Garrett?"

Jayne swallowed all the satisfying messages she could leave. "Nothing. Have fun at lunch." After she hung up the phone, she grabbed her purse and the envelope and headed to the Galleria Hotel.

Jayne found Garrett standing in a ballroom with a knot of very vocal people, among them his parents and sister. Everywhere she looked were racks of clothes, mannequins, tissue paper, plastic bags, the glitter of fallen sequins and pins. She also saw steamers and irons wielded with intense concentration by young men and women.

"I don't care for informal modeling," Rebecca Charles was saying amidst all the hubbub. "The runway is the very essence of traditional fashion shows. These contestants will expect it. How many tables you can sell if you don't have a runway shouldn't be an issue."

"I'd say not losing money is an issue!" a woman in beige linen insisted. "Besides, it isn't fair to these young designers for potential buyers not to be able to see their clothes up close. And that is the whole idea behind the modeling contest."

"I thought the idea was to discover new faces."

"Let's compromise here," Garrett said, sounding weary. "We'll have an abbreviated runway with steps at the end and the models can follow a circuit between the tables."

"It'll take forever for them to finish and change," Rebecca claimed. "We've got to keep the pace moving."

"We're not talking experienced supermodels here. They're going to be slow anyway," the woman maintained.

"That's why I don't think they should be wander-

ing among the tables. Besides, if you plan to sell as
many tables as you say you will, there won't be
room.''

Garrett picked that moment to shake his head and
saw Jayne standing near the entrance. His face
creased in a quick smile, which faded as he obviously
recalled how they'd ended their last phone conversation. Jayne tried to stay angry at him, but couldn't.
She answered his smile, then beckoned to him. He
glanced toward his mother and the other woman who
were still arguing about the runway, then quickly
strode over to her.

''I'm sorry I snapped at you earlier,'' he said, taking her elbow and ushering her out into the relative
quiet of the reception area. ''They're selecting the
clothes that will be modeled next Saturday and it's
been hectic with all the designers here. Forgive me?''

She would have forgiven him even without the
smile. ''That's okay. I know you're under a lot of
pressure.''

''But I shouldn't have taken it out on you. You
were just doing the job I'd hired you to do. Remind
me that I owe you a night out on the town when this
is all over.''

Owe. She didn't want him going out with her because he owed her. She'd thought that he...felt something for her. Yeah, gratitude.

''Did you bring the checks?'' he asked.

Jayne grimaced. ''I forgot! But here.'' She pulled
the letter out of her purse. ''I found this taped to the
back of the painting in my office.'' She hoped he
wouldn't ask how she'd made the discovery.

''It's from George,'' Garrett said as soon as he saw

the envelope. Ripping it open, he pulled out a packet of papers and a single white sheet. Jayne watched his eyes as he scanned the writing, then silently handed the paper to her.

Garrett, sell the painting. I'm leaving you the certificate of ownership papers and a list of collectors who've expressed an interest. I'm sorry. G. E. W.

Jayne could tell the note had been written in haste, yet he'd added an apology. The apology went a long way toward redeeming George in her eyes and probably Garrett's as well. That and the fact that Garrett was now free to sell the painting.

"Is it worth very much?" she asked him.

Garrett had been studying the papers. "Enough to solve our immediate financial difficulties if one of these gentlemen buys it." He exhaled and closed his eyes. "I can't believe it. We're actually going to pull this off." He grinned down at her.

Jayne was so happy and so relieved for him, that her smile was as wide as his. Their gazes caught and held. His expression changed and his eyes turned dark and smoky. *He's going to kiss me. I know it's because he's relieved and happy and I just happen to be here, but I'm going to let him kiss me anyway.* Jayne's heart picked up speed as he took a step closer.

"Jayne." Lifting his hand, he cupped her cheek, sending prickles of awareness down her neck, then bent his head.

"Garrett, there you are!" Rebecca Charles's voice rang through the reception area. "Will you please in-form Magda that we are having a bridal gown to close the show?''

With an expression of regret, Garrett dropped his hand away. Her disappointment was so keen, Jayne knew she'd need a few moments to recover.

''We can't possibly have a bridal gown.'' The woman in beige had followed Garrett's mother into the reception area.

''But everyone loves a bridal gown! Sasha, bring that one over here.'' Rebecca beckoned to Garrett's sister, who was nearly hidden by a pouf of sparkling tulle.

''Of course everyone loves a bridal gown. That's why we can't use one,'' Magda said. ''The model who wears it will have an unfair advantage over the other girls.''

Garrett's mother fussed with the dress, then looked at Garrett, her eyebrow arched. *''La la la-laaaa,''* Sasha sang and took a couple of slow, exaggerated steps. She twinkled with every movement. All she lacked was a crown and a magic wand and she could have been a fairy princess.

''She's right, Mom,'' Garrett said. ''We've got to be fair.''

''But this dress is a showstopper. Imagine the lights on all these crystals. This is every little girl's dream dress and isn't this contest all about dreams?''

Magda put a hand to her temple and gave an exaggerated sigh. ''Oh, Rebecca.''

''Oh, Magda,'' Garrett's mother mocked.

Jayne stared at the fantastic dress. Even though Sasha wasn't moving, the dress, with its constant twinkling, looked as if it was. She moved closer to see how the crystals were attached.

"It's something else, isn't it?"

"Yes," Jayne agreed simply, lifting one of what looked like twenty layers.

"Weighs a ton, too."

"So why isn't it all flat?"

"The top layer is like a loose net and each layer under it has smaller holes so the crystals show through and it stays puffy."

It was the three-dimensional effect that made the dress so unusual.

"You know, if this had been made by a name designer, it would cost a fortune, but I sure wouldn't want to wear it in the show."

Jayne looked up sharply. "Why not?"

"This is a modeling contest," Sasha said. "Everybody would be looking at the dress instead of at me."

"You see?" Magda gestured in triumph. "Even your own daughter admits that it wouldn't be a good idea to model this dress."

"Look at this work." Rebecca grabbed a handful of tulle and crystal. "This is Diego's second year to show for the Fashion Council and it will be his last because by this time next year, he will be too famous for you. Do you really want to be known for not recognizing the hottest young designer to come out of Houston in years?"

Magda gave her a sharp look and stared at the dress. "You have a point. Sasha, if you weren't a professional, I'd ask you to wear it."

"It's too short for me anyway." She looked up and met Jayne's eyes. "Let Jayne wear it."

"Me?"

"Who?" Magda asked.

"Jayne, our business manager." Rebecca swept an assessing glance over her before taking the dress from Sasha and holding it up next to Jayne. "The length is right for you."

"Diego must have been making this dress for someone of her height," Magda said.

"What do you say, Garrett? Acceptable compromise?"

"It's up to Jayne." He regarded her with a slight smile.

They thought she could actually model? Jayne was almost dizzy with happiness—or hunger. "I'd love to!"

But even Jayne's newly svelte figure was a tight squeeze for the bridal gown. The bodice was fitted and the zipper barely closed. She caught Diego's concerned look in the mirror, but he said nothing. Jayne knew why—he wanted his dress shown, even if the model burst out of it. Well, this model wouldn't burst. This model wasn't going to eat until after Saturday. Besides, she had a painting to sell.

"I'm sorry to stick that with you," Garrett had said after she'd tried on the bridal gown and he was walking her through the hotel lobby.

"I'll have it appraised, then find a dealer. You'll be out the commission, though."

"Don't worry about it. If we had more time, then maybe we could learn how to sell it ourselves. Right now, I'll be happy if we get what we paid for it." They reached the lobby doors. Garrett shoved his hands into his pockets, something he rarely did. "And, look, Jayne, about this wedding dress...don't let them bully you into getting involved with this craziness. You've got plenty to do at the agency."

Jayne had been digging in her purse for her car keys and looked up to find his expression serious. "They didn't bully me."

"You weren't exactly in a position to say 'no' gracefully."

"It's fine. I want to do it."

"Fashion shows aren't like you think they'll be. Everyone will be staring at you."

"They'll be staring at the dress."

"And you'll be in the dress. I've seen models get stage fright before. I don't want you to be uncomfortable."

"Garrett, there'll be a rehearsal. Don't worry about me." She smiled and he made an attempt to answer it, but didn't quite succeed.

"Just remember that you can quit at any time."

"Okay."

Now he did smile. "How about dinner tonight?"

"Are you kidding?" Jayne laughed. "I can't eat. That dress was a little too snug. I'm hitting the gym for an extra half hour on the treadmill, then having a lettuce leaf and bouillon for dinner."

It was only after she was on the treadmill that Jayne realized that Garrett had been trying to discourage her from modeling the bridal gown. Didn't he think she could? He thought Sylvia could. And if Sylvia could, she could. Jayne adjusted the resistance on the treadmill and decided to skip dinner.

* * *

"I told you I would handle the sale of the painting, and I have. I found a dealer who agreed to cut her commission, since we gave her the names of potential buyers. She contacted them, and as we speak, there is a discreet bidding war going on. You may even come out of this with a profit."

Garrett stared at the brittle face across the desk. Something was wrong and had been wrong for several days. Since Jayne had agreed to model the bridal gown, in fact. The emotional closeness between them was gone and he didn't know why. He only knew he wanted it back. "I am busy and so are you," he said. "But not so busy I can't be informed of the agency's financial business."

"It isn't necessary to keep tabs on me. I'm not George Windom."

If he hadn't known something was wrong before, then he would have known it after that crack. That wasn't like Jayne. "You know I trust you. Is something wrong?" he asked after a moment.

"No, nothing."

His gaze swept over her face and white-knuckled hands, which clasped a pen, taking in the grayish circles under her eyes and her attempts to camouflage them with makeup. Her lips, carefully lined and filled in with color, were pressed tightly together. She was a poster girl for stress.

"You need a break," he decided. "I'm taking you out to Nicky V's tonight." He smiled coaxingly. "Wear your black suit?"

She stared at him and when she spoke her voice was flat. "The black suit is too big for me now."
Garrett felt a pang. He had fond memories of that suit.

Reaching across the desk, he covered her clenched hands with his. "Jayne, I know you've lost weight. You've been working too hard. This agency should be my worry, not yours."

"But you don't have to worry. I'm taking care of the financial side so you can concentrate on the contest."

"But running back and forth between here and the hotel is obviously too much for you."

Her eyes widened and there was a slight tremble in the clenched hands beneath his before she pulled them away. "Why do you say that?"

Slowly Garrett straightened. "You're stressed out and you aren't yourself."

"I'm hungry."

"Then let's go to lunch." Garrett glanced at his watch, surprised to note that it was only ten o'clock.

"No! It's hard enough to lose weight without you dragging me off to Italian restaurants."

Garrett was seriously alarmed. "Jayne, you don't need to lose weight."

"How else do you expect me to get into that bridal gown?" she cried, her face contorted.

He'd known something like this was bound to happen. As soon as his sister had suggested Jayne model that gown, he'd had a premonition of disaster. The sweetly passionate Jayne he'd known was gone. He'd watched her studying the modeling contestants day after day, undoubtedly comparing herself. He'd seen her hands tremble when she reached for a water glass, had seen her sway and grab for the nearest table or chair. Watched her try to turn herself into his sister or his mother. He hated this business.

"I don't expect you to get into the bridal gown and in fact, I wish you wouldn't. You're killing yourself for no good reason." He stood and pointed to the computer. "In fact, with the shape you're in, it wouldn't surprise me to find that your work is full of mistakes. Tired and hungry people make mistakes, Jayne. Am I going to have to hire an accountant to go over your work?"

"M-my work is fine."

He'd shaken her. Good. She needed shaking.

"Is it? I'm not sure." He drew a deep breath. "Tell them you've changed your mind about wearing the dress, then take the rest of today off. Go home, rest and eat something."

She stared at him, then shook her head. Sighing, he rested his knuckles on her desk, then pushed away. "I wish you'd never agreed to wear that stupid dress!"

He couldn't seriously believe that she'd back out only two days before the contest! Not after she'd come this far. Besides, the rehearsal was tomorrow. Once he saw her in the dress, he'd change his mind. He'd see that she wasn't a Plain Jane any longer. And, maybe, the next time he asked her to dinner, it would be because he thought she was a desirable woman and not a drab accountant he "owed."

"Jayne, I can't believe we're actually here." Sylvia squeezed her hand in the dressing room.

"I know. Good luck today, Sylvia."

Jayne was helping her set up the area where she would change into the outfits she was modeling. Last night had taught everyone the importance of having everything ready to throw on, because there wasn't as much time to change as the models expected.

Last night hardly counted for Jayne, though. She hadn't worn the dress because there just weren't any spare hands to help her into it. Since she wasn't competing, she just walked out at the end of the show and stood at the end of the runway. Garrett had been there, silent and unsmiling. Well, tomorrow night he'd smile, she'd thought. Tomorrow night, he'd be dazzled. Then she'd executed a turn like the one Sandor had taught Sylvia, only her feet stopped, but her head didn't. The room spun and Jayne felt herself stumble.

Strong arms caught her and Garrett's harsh voice was in her ear.

"When was the last time you ate?"

"I just tripped, that's all," she protested, irritated. But Garrett had helped her down the stairs and over to the hospitality table where he'd made her drink two glasses of juice.

Jayne had felt every calorie as it slid down her throat, but she had felt better afterward. She wasn't going to make the same mistake today, though. She'd eaten breakfast and a light lunch, and had watched the photo sessions. Now it was time for the fashion show.

The ballroom was full—as full as Magda had predicted. She and Rebecca and James Charles were jointly hosting the evening and introducing the models and the clothes. When they heard the music start, Jayne wished Sylvia luck once more, then went to the room that had been set aside for her.

There was the dress, hanging against the mirror in

all its glittery splendor. Three other people were in the room, apparently to assist her.

"Go ahead and get into the dress first, then we'll do your makeup." That seemed backward to Jayne, and too, she felt funny undressing and standing in her underwear in front of everyone, but they seemed to expect her to do so.

She gamely stepped into the dress and Diego, himself, zipped her up. Jayne was afraid to breathe, but the zipper closed without a problem. Diego smiled at her in the mirror, and helped her up the pedestal. Then he began twitching the dress and checking the hems of the myriad layers. Jayne felt like a fairy princess. A relieved fairy princess. The dress fit. It had all been worth it.

She stared at herself in the mirror, hardly able to believe she was the same woman who had spent her twenty-eighth birthday with a calculator. She'd wanted to jazz up her life, and she had. She'd also wanted to be the sort of woman who would be noticed by a man like Garrett. Imagining his face when he saw her walking down that runway made her smile. At first, he'd look thunderstruck, then his smile would grow and his eyes would fill with love. Love. Jayne swallowed. It was okay to admit that she loved Garrett now. She couldn't before because there was no chance of him loving her back. But after today, he'd finally see how she could fit in with his family. He wouldn't have to be ashamed of her. When they were out together, women wouldn't stare and wonder how Jayne had ended up with a handsome man like Garrett.

Diego straightened and moved around to the back

of the dress, arranging the layers of crystals as he went. The doorway was now visible in the mirror. As if her thoughts had conjured him, Jayne noticed Garrett standing there. For a moment, she saw his unguarded expression in the mirror and it was everything she'd hoped to see. The makeup artist swished the cape around her and her eyes met Garrett's.

He watched as the artist quickly applied blush and shadow to her face. With each layer of makeup, Garrett's face grew harder until he finally left. What was wrong? Jayne gazed at herself in the mirror, no longer seeing a fairy princess but a woman who was trying to be something she wasn't. The eye makeup was exaggerated and her cheeks were too pink.

"Don't worry, hon, you're going to be wearing a veil, so we made you up heavier than usual. Your face wouldn't have shown up otherwise."

The hairstylist attacked her next, randomly pinning her curls so some remained down. Then Diego unwrapped a headpiece that looked like swirls of crystals were suspended in the air, sparkling above her head and showering over her face. Attached to and floating from her nape was a swath of veil so long that Jayne couldn't see the end of it. With a flourish, they removed the cape.

Jayne stared at herself. She looked awful. She didn't look like a fairy princess, she looked like the wicked witch. There was silence in the room. Awful, hideous silence. At least they weren't laughing at her. But the audience would. That was what Garrett had been trying to tell her. No matter what she did, she would never look good enough, never be accepted by them. She couldn't go out on that stage and listen to the other models snicker and the audience laugh. She couldn't.

With a sob, Jayne jumped off the pedestal.

"Hey! Where are you going? They haven't played your cue yet."

"I...have to go to the bathroom!"

Jayne gathered as much of Diego's carefully arranged layers as she could and ran out the door, ignoring their dumbfounded expressions. The veil streamed behind her. Jayne would have reeled it in, but then she would have had to drop the dress, so she continued to run, hoping no one would follow her.

She reached the reception area outside the ballroom and panicked when she saw herself in the gilt-framed mirrors. The dress was huge. Enormous. And heavy. The veil must be twenty feet long, and the headpiece... Well, forget it.

How was she supposed to escape? Riding the escalator was out and she doubted her ability to get all the way inside the elevator.

"Jayne!" It was Garrett. No. She couldn't face him. Frantically Jayne looked for someplace to hide, but there wasn't much around that could conceal the dress. She stepped behind a pillar and covered her face with her hands.

"Jayne, what are you doing?" His voice sounded next to her.

"Hiding."

He chuckled. "You aren't doing a very good job."

"I'm not doing a good job at anything."

"Jayne, look at me."

How could she look at him? She felt him tugging

at her veil and then lifting the heavy crystal layer away from her face.

"You're smearing your makeup."

Jayne dropped her hands. If he thought she was smearing it now, just wait until she started crying.

"What's wrong?" His voice was strong and tender and concerned all at the same time and it was too much for her. Heedless of his tuxedo, she buried her face against his lapel. "Is it stage fright? You don't have to go out there, Jayne."

"It's not stage fright...I don't want to be laughed at."

"Laughed at?"

"Yes. I saw how they looked at me in the dressing room. No one said a word because they were all trying not to laugh. Everyone's been making fun of me, haven't they?"

"No." He sounded so certain. But...

"I saw your face, too." She looked up at him.

"What did you see?"

"You—you were disgusted or—or angry."

"Or both."

Jayne tried to pull away, but Garrett held her fast. "Shall I tell you why?"

"Because I don't look good enough? Because I can't be like your family and the other models?"

He shook his head. "Because you looked so happy. Happier than I've seen you in weeks and all because you'd starved yourself until you'd nearly fainted, and had someone doing your hair and putting on your makeup."

"But—"

"I never wanted you to be like my family! I loved

you because you weren't like them and then you
started turning into them and I couldn't stop you.
Tonight, I couldn't see any of the beautiful Jayne I'd
fallen in love with.''

Love? Jayne's mouth fell open. Beautiful?

''I've missed her.'' Smiling wistfully, Garrett
cupped her cheek, echoing his gesture from a week
ago.

This time, his mother didn't interrupt their kiss.
The instant his lips met hers, Jayne shuddered at what
she'd nearly lost—and which wasn't a sure thing even
now.

''You love me?'' she asked, when it became obvious that the dress precluded any serious kissing.

Garrett hesitated. ''I love the Jayne who wore the
black suit to Nicky V's and talked half the night
away. I love the Jayne who is passionate about numbers and assumes that I understand everything she
tells me. And, I do love the Jayne who learned enough
about fashion to snag Darnia and Brynn.''

''That was an accident,'' she confessed in a mum-
ble.

''A happy accident, except that it seemed to trigger
this obsession with your appearance.''

''Garrett, I'm so sorry. I've been a complete idiot.
I just—''

''Couldn't get past the way I look?'' His voice was
bitter. ''Is that the only reason you're attracted to
me?''

''No! How could you think that?'' Horrified, she
answered her own question. ''Because that's the way
I've been acting.''

She searched his face and saw the endearing need

for reassurance. Smiling, she smoothed the hair back from his forehead. ''You are incredibly good-looking, but that just became one part of you for me. You're kind and smart and…and you're loyal to your family and friends and in your business dealings. People don't think much about loyalty anymore, but I think it counts for a lot. I'm sorry you thought… Oh, Garrett, I love you so much and I was afraid you wouldn't love me the way I was!''

''Looks aren't forever, Jayne, but the qualities we love about each other are. Can you remember that?''

''After tonight, how could I forget? I can't believe I've been so obsessed with the way I look.''

''Don't blame yourself. We do foolish things when we fall in love.''

''I don't see that you've done any stupid things.''

''Not telling you the instant I knew I was in love with you and wanted to spend the rest of my life with you wasn't too bright. I could have saved us a lot of time.''

Jayne felt dizzy and this time it wasn't from hunger. ''You…you…are you…?''

''Yes, Jayne, I'm asking you to marry me.'' He waved an arm at her dress and his formal attire. ''It seems to fit in with the theme.''

''Oh, Garrett!'' And this time when Jayne flung her arms around him, not even the dress could keep them apart.

Heedless of thousands of crystals, Garrett crushed her to him. Jayne was instantly transported to the night in the parking lot when the kiss was so perfect she thought she'd imagined it. Garrett's lips moved over hers as he whispered her name, holding her close and murmuring words of love between kisses. The sound of the wedding march broke them apart.

"My cue!"

He searched her face. "Do you still want to model the dress?"

"Oh, I have to! I can't let Diego down." Jayne took off running. "Watch my veil for me!"

Breathless, she arrived backstage in time to register Diego's relieved face. He quickly jerked her headpiece back into place and then he and Garrett stuffed Jayne through the narrow doorway entrance to the runway.

As Jayne stepped out into the lights, there was a gasp and applause. She was momentarily blinded by the spotlight, then felt a strong arm steady her as Garrett placed her hand in the crook of his elbow. "I'm here. After all, a bride does need a groom."

And together, they closed the show.

If you enjoyed what you just read,
then we've got an offer you can't resist!

Take 2 bestselling love stories FREE!

Plus get a FREE surprise gift!

Coming Next Month

#3559 THE ONE-WEEK MARRIAGE Renee Roszel
Isabel has always played down her looks around her boss. But now he
wants her to pretend to be his "wife" for a week, and she knows, as she
sheds her drab feathers, Gabe will be in for the shock of his life!

#3560 TO TAME A BRIDE Susan Fox
Maddie St. John is everything Lincoln Coryell despises in a woman—
she's glamorous, socially privileged and devotes all her time to looking
good! Linc has to admit she's certainly gorgeous. But when they're
stranded alone together, he discovers that Maddie isn't just a spoiled
socialite. She has a loving heart—and Linc could be the man to tame
her!

Rebel Brides: *Two rebellious cousins—and the men who tame them!*

#3561 FARELLI'S WIFE Lucy Gordon
When Franco Farelli had married Joanne's cousin, Joanne had
graciously stepped aside, her love for Franco kept secret. Now he was
begging her to stay, if only for his motherless son's sake. But Joanne
needed to believe his desire for her wasn't because she resembled her
cousin, but because he wanted her for herself....

Kids & Kisses: *Where kids and kisses go hand in hand!*

#3562 BACHELOR COWBOY Patricia Knoll
Luke had been an infuriating puzzle to Shannon since their first
prickly meeting. Now he was desperate for her help, having been left in
charge of his baby nephew. As she taught him how to take care of little
Cody, Shannon saw that Luke's defenses were melting—just like her
heart....

Marriage Ties: *The four Kelleher women, bound together by family
and love.*

HARLEQUIN FIVE DECADES OF ROMANCE CELEBRATES

In July 1999 Harlequin Superromance®
brings you *The Lyon Legacy*—a
brand-new 3-in-1 book from popular
authors Peg Sutherland, Roz Denny Fox
& Ruth Jean Dale

3 stories for the price of 1!

Join us as we celebrate
Harlequin's 50th Anniversary!

Look for these other
Harlequin Superromance®
titles wherever books are sold July 1999:

A COP'S GOOD NAME (#846)
by Linda Markowiak
THE MAN FROM HIGH MOUNTAIN (#848)
by Kay David
HER OWN RANGER (#849)
by Anne Marie Duquette
SAFE HAVEN (#850)
by Evelyn A. Crowe
JESSIE'S FATHER (#851)
by C. J. Carmichael